ARMITAGE TRAIL

SCARFACE

FIRST PUBLISHED 1930

BLACKMASK.COM EDITION 2005

ISBN: 1-59654-212-8

BLACKMASK ONLINE IS A DIVISION OF DISRUPTIVE PUBLISHING, INC.

chapter 1

Tony Guarino, destined to be the greatest of all America's notorious gang leaders, was eighteen when he committed his first serious crime. And the cause, as is so often the case, was a woman.

But what a woman! Standing there in the dark alley that gave access to the street from the sheet-iron stage door of the cheap burlesque house, Tony could visualize her easily. A tall, stately blonde with golden hair, and a pink and white complexion and long, graceful white legs. From the audience he had watched those legs many times while she danced her way through the performance and they never failed to give him a tingly thrill that left him rather breathless.

The stage door opened suddenly, letting a square of yellow light out on the throng of dark, overdressed men and older boys waiting, like so many wolves, for their night's prey. Then the door slammed shut with a dull clang, plunging the alley into darkness again, and a girl swished rapidly through the crowd, seemingly oblivious of the hands that reached out to detain her and of the raucous voices that brazenly offered invitations.'

It was she! Nobody but Vyvyan Lovejoy used that particular heavy, sensuous perfume. Tony plunged after her, toward the lights and noise that indicated the street.

She paused at the sidewalk, a lithe, slender figure, overdressed in a vivid green ensemble suit with a skirt that was both too short and too tight, and glittering with much imitation jewelry. People with a proper perspective would have recognized her for the false and dangerous beacon of allure that she was, but to Tony she was marvelous, something to worship and possess.

He moved up beside her and took off his cap. That was one of the things he had learned from the movies, the only social tutor he had ever had.

"Good evening, Miss Lovejoy."

She turned on him the face he thought so lovely. He couldn't see that its complexion was as false as her jewelry; couldn't see the ravages of dissipation that lay beneath the paint and powder; didn't notice the hard cruel lines about the garish mouth, nor the ruthless greed in the painted, rather large nose. As she surveyed him, contempt came into her hardened bold face and her greenish eyes took on a strange glitter.

"You!" she said. "Again."

"No—yet." Tony laughed at what he thought a brilliant witticism. "And I'm goin' to keep on bein' here every night till you gimme a date."

The girl laughed, a short, sharp, mirthless sound that was more like a grunt.

"Can y'imagine the nerve o' th' punk?" she demanded, as though addressing an audience, but her cold green eyes bored straight into Tony's defiant black ones. "Just a mere child without even a car and tryin' to date *me* up. Say, kid, do you know who my boy friend is?"

"No, and I don't care," retorted Tony with the passion-inspired recklessness of the Latin. "But I'm goin' to be."

"Well, it's Al Spingola."

Something inside of Tony suddenly went cold. Al Spingola was one of the city's important gang leaders, a ruthless man with a big income, a lot of hoodlums who were loyal to him because they feared him and he paid them well, and a quick trigger finger himself. A dangerous man!

"Aw, I bet he ain't so hot," answered Tony stubbornly.

"Well, maybe not," conceded Vyvyan, "but at least he can give a girl sonip'm more substantial than kisses.... Whenever you get a flock o' dough, kid, an' a big car, why come around and then maybe I'll talk to you."

She laughed again and stepped out to the curb as a big shiny limousine drew up with a rush and stopped. Tony started after her. Then he paused as he recognized the man at the wheel of that car. It was Al Spingola! A heavy-set, swarthy man with hard, reckless dark eyes and a cruel mouth with thick, brutal lips, handsomely dressed in gray and with an enormous diamond glittering in his tie. As everyone knew, the most important part of his dress lay snugly against his hip, a snub-nosed blue steel revolver seldom seen, but when it was, sure to be heard and felt by somebody. Tony realized that for him to say another word to Vyvyan then would be certain death. Not at the moment, of course, because that place was too public. But within a few days his body would be found in an alley somewhere.

Spingola glanced at Tony as the girl climbed into the car. And the boy felt cold and nervous until the expensive machine purred away at high speed. Spingola, like other of his ilk, always drove at high speed, thereby lessening his availability as a target.

Tony watched the car race away, then he put on his cap and lighted a cigarette. Walking around the corner to a poolroom which was his main hang-out, he sat down in one of the high chairs to think out this thing that was his first adult problem. Usually his mind, even though uneducated, was alert and precise, its processes rapid and sound. But now it was dulled by the gnawing, overpowering hunger of his first great passion. Of course he had had any number of affairs with the neighborhood girls; no *boy* as good-looking as he could help that. But somehow they hadn't satisfied him. He wanted something bigger, more mature than the shallow, entirely physical emotion that these girls offered. He was shockingly old for his age, as is almost every boy from such an environment. He looked twenty-five with his wise eyes, cynical mouth and well-developed beard that left a heavy pattern on his swarthy cheeks. And he possessed more actual knowledge of mankind and its vagaries than most men acquire in a lifetime. You could have set him down flat broke in any city in the world and he wouldn't have missed a meal. Nor would he have needed to steal; stealing was the way of people without brains. He held a contempt for thieves; particularly those of the petty larceny variety.

"Say!" whispered a surly voice in his ear.

Tony looked up into a rat face topped by a dirty, rumpled checked cap.

"Well?" he said coldly.

"Some of us are goin' out and knock over some gas stations," answered the other boy hoarsely. "Want to come along?"

"No."

"It'll be an even split all round."

"*No,*" I said. I ain't riskin' a pinch for a coupla bucks."

"Aw, there'll be more'n that, Tony. All them places got fifty, sixty bucks layin' around. An' there'll only be about four of us."

"*Screw!*" snarled Tony. "Before I paste you one."

The other boy hurried away, muttering to himself. To the other boys who loafed around this poolroom, Tony was a puzzle. They never became intimate with him the way they did with each other. Somehow it just never occurred to them to do so. They realized the difference; so did he. But neither of them knew the reason. A psychologist would have explained it by saying that Tony had a "mental percentage" on the others, that it was the difference between a man destined for leadership and men destined to run in the pack.

Most of the boys in the neighborhood made illegal forays nightly. Never in their own ward, of course, because that would have alienated the alderman. Whereas when they made raids only in outside wards, their own alderman—in case they were arrested—would come down to the station, tell what fine reputations they had in their neighborhood, and help get them out. Then on election day, each hoodlum not only voted fifteen or twenty times, but hordes of them swept through the ward and threatened everybody with dire reprisals if the alderman were not re-elected by a handsome majority. And the people, realizing the truth of these threats, re-elected the alderman, even though they knew he was a grand old thug.

Tony always refused to join these nightly expeditions for ill-gotten gains. "Petty larceny stuff," as he contemptuously referred to their depredations, did not interest him. He wanted to be a "big shot," a leader, perhaps a politician. He had a hunger for command, for power, for wealth. And he meant to have it all. In the meantime, though he had no job that anybody knew of and although he refused to fall in with the criminal ways of his neighbors, he dressed better than they and seemed to have all the money he needed. Many of the boys wondered about that, but inasmuch as he chose to volunteer nothing, it was likely to remain a mystery for, in that neighborhood, one did not inquire into the source of income of even an intimate friend. And Tony had no intimate friends.

There was a sudden commotion at the front door of the poolroom and several burly men came in. Some of the people already present tried to escape by the back door, only to be confronted and driven back in by other burly men coming in there. Detectives, of course, going to look over the crowd.

Knowing that they had nothing on him, Tony watched with faint amusement and a large sense of virtue while the dicks went through the poorly lighted, smoke-filled room, tapping hips, asking questions, occasionally bestowing a hard, backhand slap on the ugly mouth of some hoodlum who tried to talk back. As he had expected, they made no move to molest him.

"This kid's all right," said a man he recognized as Lieutenant Grady from the neighborhood station. "He's Ben Guarino's brother."

"That don't mean anything," retorted a burly, cold-eyed man whose hard-boiled demeanor identified him as from headquarters.

"Does to Tony!" snapped Grady. "We've never heard of him bein' outside, the law yet, either in this ward or any other."

"Thanks, Lieutenant!" smiled Tony. "Can't I buy a cigar for you and the boys?"

They all laughed at that. Not a man of them but what was old enough to be his father, yet he called them "boys" and they liked it. With all the poise and self-possession of a judge on his own bench, Tony led the crowd of officers to the front of the poolroom and purchased cigars for them all. Then they exchanged cheery "Good nights" with him and departed. Already Tony had learned the manifold advantage of having a good "rep" with the cops. Also he knew the great power that came from having people in one's debt, even for such little things as cigars. Tony seldom accepted a favor from anyone, but if he did, he always tried to return one twice as big, thus removing his moral debt to them and making them indebted to him. He had the mind and soul of a master politician.

Tony suddenly realized that the stuffy, smoke-filled atmosphere of the poolroom had given him a headache, and decided to go home. Except for occasional oases like the poolroom, the neighborhood was a desert of gloom and deserted frowsiness. Street lights were infrequent and those that existed were of the old-fashioned, sputtering type that, like some people, made a lot of noise but accomplished little. It hadn't rained that night, yet there was an unhealthy dampness about. The dingy old buildings, with their ground-floor windows boarded up like blind eyes, seemed to hover malevolently over the narrow, dirty streets. One street that served as a pushcart market by day was littered with boxes and papers and heaps of reeking refuse. An occasional figure, either hunting or hunted, skulked along. Infrequently, a car raced past, awakening echoes that could be heard for blocks through the quiet streets. Over all hung a brooding stir of ever-present menace, an indefinable something that made sensitive strangers to the neighborhood suddenly look back over their shoulders for no good reason.

This was the setting of gangland, its spawning place, . its lair and one of its principal hunting grounds. It was also Tony's neighborhood, the only environment he had ever known. But he could not see that a great scheme of circumstances, a web much too intricate for him to understand, had gradually been shaping his destiny since the day of his birth, that it was as difficult for him to keep from being a gangster as it was for a Crown Prince to keep from becoming King.

Tony reached the little grocery store that his parents owned, and above which the family lived, passed to the door beyond, inserted his key and clattered up the dirty, uncarpeted steps. A light was on in the dining room, which also served as the parlor. Seated in an old rocker which had been patched with wire, sat Ben Guarino reading the paper, his blue uniformed legs and heavy, square-toed black shoes resting on the dirty red and white checked tablecloth. His revolver, resting in its holster, hung suspended by the cartridge belt from the back of another rickety chair upon which rested his uniform coat and cap.

As Tony came in, Ben looked up. He was a stocky chap in the middle twenties with a brutal mouth and jaw and defiant dark eyes that usually held a baleful glitter. For a number of reasons, all of which he kept to himself, Tony felt that his brother was going to be a big success as a policeman. To Tony, the only difference between a policeman and a gangster was a badge. They both came from the same sort of neighborhoods, had about the same education and ideas, usually knew each other before and after their paths diverged, and always got along well together if the gangsters had enough money.

"Where you been so late?" demanded Ben truculently.

"What the hell's it to you?" retorted Tony, then remembering the favor he was going to ask, became peaceable. "I didn't mean to be cross, Ben. But I got a nasty headache."

"Down to that O'Hara joint again, I s'pose?"

"Well, a fellow's got to have some place to go in the evening. And the only other place is some dance hall with a lot o' them cheap, silly broads."

"Gettin' choosy about your women, now, eh?"

"Yes."

"Well, that's right," answered Ben with a grin. "There's nothin'll take a man to the top—or to the bottom—faster than a high-toned woman eggin' him on." Suddenly his feet struck the floor and he leaned forward, his eyes boring straight into those of his brother. "Say, what's this I hear about you deliverin' packages for Smoky Joe?"

"Well?"

"Didn't you know there was dope in them packages?"

"No, I didn't. But now that I do, it's goin' to cost him more."

"You let that stuff alone."

"Oh, all right. I s'pose some cop belly-ached to you about it. Well, he can have that little graft, if he wants it. I got other things I can do."

"Yes, I guess you have," agreed Ben drily, "from all I hear. So you been a lookout down at Mike Rafferty's gamblin' joint, too?"

"Yes. And why not? That's a decent way of makin' a few bucks. Would you rather have me out pullin' stick-ups like the rest of the guys in the neighborhood?"

"Of course not." He leaned forward and spoke seriously. "Don't ever get in no serious trouble, Tony; it would ruin me at headquarters."

"I won't. Don't worry about me. You got enough to do to watch your own step."

"What do you mean?"

"Nothin'," answered Tony casually with a smile, enjoying the sudden fear that had come into his brother's face. "That's just a friendly tip from a fellow that knows more than you think he does."

"Who?" demanded Ben hoarsely.

"Me." Tony grinned again and flipped his cigarette ashes on the bare floor. "Say, Ben, can I have your car tomorrow night?"

"No. I'm usin' it myself. That's my night off."

"How about the next night?"

"No. You'd prob'ly get in trouble with it. Kids and cars don't go together."

"All right. I'll have one o' my own pretty soon and I'm goin' to get it as easy as you got that one."

With which parting shot, Tony went in to bed, slamming the door shut behind him. How a fellow making a hundred and fifty a month could acquire honestly a car that cost nearly three thousand dollars was too much for Tony. But then all policemen had big cars, and captains had strings of apartment buildings and sent their children to European finishing schools.

The strange quiet that momentarily descended over the Guarino household at this time of night was balm to Tony. It was the only period of the twenty-four hours that he could spend at home without feeling that he was about to go crazy. The rest of the time it was noise... noise... noise.... He wondered if other people's homes were as uninviting and repellent; all those he had ever seen were.

He undressed quickly and climbed into the grimy bed which he and Ben shared. He wanted to sleep before Ben came in so that they couldn't argue any more. But his mind was racing and it kept swinging around to Vyvyan Lovejoy. Even to think about her made him alternately hot and cold all over and left him trembling with anticipation. He *would* have her; nobody could stop him—not even Al Spingola.

The fact that the woman he wanted belonged to another made not the slightest difference to Tony. All life was a battle and the strongest man got the gravy. Anyway, she had said she would talk to him if he had a car and some money. Well, he'd get 'em both, and be back at that stage door tomorrow night.

chapter 2

Promptly at ten-thirty the next night Tony Guarino entered the dark alley that led to the sheet-iron stage door of the tawdry Gaiety Theatre. And he swaggered a little as he walked. He felt big and powerful and grand, an unnatural exultation due partly to his having visited three saloons on the way over—an unusual occurrence for him—but due mainly to the fact that he was ready for anything. At the curb stood a fast and expensive sport roadster that ordinarily saw service in more nefarious enterprises. He had rented it for the evening—just why he didn't know. According to the people who were in that racket, stealing a car was about the easiest of all crimes, both to commit and to get away with; it was the way ninety per cent of criminals started. But he didn't intend to be pinched the very first time that Vyvyan honored him with her company—because she was going to go with him tonight, even if she didn't know it yet—so he had rented the roadster for the night.

In his pants pocket bulged a wad of bills that totaled two hundred dollars—all the money he had in the world. It was so arranged that a crisp new bill of $100 denomination served as "wrapper" on the outside. The inside, a few fives but mostly ones, expanded the $100 note until the roll looked to be worth ten times its real value.

Thus he had everything she had asked for. But he also had something else. In his right hand side coat pocket rested an ugly blue steel revolver he had bought that afternoon. He had never carried a gun before and he found in it a big thrill. It gave one a sense of security and power, of equality with all the world. Why, with this revolver in his pocket he was just as good as Al Spingola. Thus

Tony argued himself into a state of exaltation and high courage. But deep in his own soul he wondered just how he would act if he should be forced into an actual life-and-death encounter with Spingola.

Vyvyan came prancing out a little early, glittering and fragrant as usual, an enormous picture hat framing her hard face.

"Well, fer Gawd's sake!" she exclaimed when she saw him. "Mary's little lamb is on the job again."

"Betcher life," grinned Tony. "An' I got the car an' a flock o' dough, like you wanted."

"You have?" she said mockingly. "Well, that puts little Johnny at the head of the class."

Tony's grin faded suddenly and he grabbed her arm.

"Listen, sister, don't try to kid me!" he snarled. "You an' I are goin' steppin' tonight."

"Yeah?"

"Yeah! So you might as well make up your mind to it and come along."

"Well," she said wearily, "I'm not to see Al till tomorrow night so I s'pose I might as well take a chance on you now. But I don't want anybody to see us, so that he'll hear about it." She shivered slightly. "Al's dangerous, kid. So drive to the corner of Taylor and Sangamon and wait for me there. I'll take a taxi and be along within five minutes."

"You're not giving me the run-around?"

"Absolutely not. I'll be there'."

"Well, you better," said Tony darkly. "Or I'll be back tomorrow night and shoot up the place."

He entered the roadster and roared away, feeling very important. At the appointed corner, he waited nervously, muttering dire threats to himself. But she came, and hurriedly climbed in beside him. The narrow confines of the roadster caused their thighs to touch for their whole length and he felt a sudden thrill from the contact. When she looked up at him suddenly with a queer light in her greenish eyes, he knew she had felt his revolver.

"S'all right, baby," he grinned reassuringly. "I won't use it unless I have to."

He drove her to a North Side restaurant that was noted for its discretion. Seated opposite each other in a small private dining room on the second floor, they consumed a fine and expensive meal, and two bottles of champagne. Those were the days when real champagne could be had at almost any restaurant.

The meal over, and with only another bottle and glasses on the table, Tony moved his chair around beside Vyvyan's. She had progressed nicely and by now had reached the stage where she occasionally blew a long breath upward along her face with a loud "Whoosh!" as if to blow her hair out of her eyes.

"Well, kid, how do you feel?" asked Tony, reaching for her hand.

"Kinda warm," she giggled.

"So do I."

When he took her home shortly before five in the morning, she kissed him good night and climbed out of the roadster with a heavy sigh.

"Boy, you sure can love!" she said weakly and, tottered into her cheap hotel.

Tony arose at noon that day. A close shave with plenty of powder at the end made him look a little less haggard. There was a curious sense of elation singing within him. At last he had mastered a real woman, a woman much older and more experienced than he. He had found, too, that it was the mastering of another that he enjoyed in love. The thirst for power was almost a mania with him.' And the fact that circumstances and conditions made it so that he had no right to ever expect to have any made him want it all the more.

His sister, Rosie, a tall, pretty girl of sixteen, cooked a meal for him. The six other children were at school.

He ate hurriedly and in silence. There was so much to do now.

Clattering down the stairs, his mother's raucous, commanding shout reached his ears. He hesitated a moment, then entered the store, looking sullen and defiant. Mrs. Guarino was a squat, wrinkled Italian woman of fifty, with a figure like a loosely packed sack tied tightly in the middle, dressed in a shapeless, indescribable gray wrapper whose waistline was invisible from the front due to her breasts dripping over it. Her unbobbed gray hair was drawn up all around and screwed into a tight knot atop her head. Heavy, plain gold ear-rings hung from holes punched through the lobes of her ears. Yet despite her ugliness and barbaric appearance, her features were good, indicating native intelligence and honesty. Carlotta Guarino was a good citizen. If only she could have made her children as good citizens as were she and their father—but then that was impossible, though she didn't see why, nor did they.

"Where were you so late?" she demanded in rapid-fire Italian. "It was after five when you came in."

"Aw, I was talkin' business with somebody," answered Tony in English.

"What kind of business could you talk at that time of the morning?" she demanded again in Italian. "You come home earlier. You be a good boy like Ben and don't get us into any trouble."

"All right," assented Tony and hurried out, relieved at escaping after so short a grilling.

That was the way it always went, reproaches, recriminations, cautions. She and his father could think of more things he shouldn't do. It never occurred to him that they were endeavoring to implant in him their own code of ethics and honesty. Their crudeness of expression kept him from realizing that. Even if he had realized it, he wouldn't have accepted it. Because, while he loved his parents with the fierce, clan-love of the Latin, he did not respect their ideas. There were many logical reasons for that—their inability to learn English well, their inability to keep step with the times and country, their bewilderment—even after twenty years—at the great nation which they had chosen for their new home, the fact that even with his father working hard every day and his mother tending the little store they had been able to make only a bare living for the large family. So why should he accept their ideas on ethics? Where had those ideas gotten them? Tony didn't intend to live in squalor like this all his life; he meant to be a big shot. Thus another decent home spawned another gangster, as inevitably as an oyster creates a pearl.

There were other factors, of course, that contributed strongly in making Tony a gangster. His attitude toward the law, for instance. His first contact with it had come at the age of *six* when, hungry, he had snatched a pear off a push-cart and a policeman had chased him. Thus, from the first, he had known the law as an enemy instead of a protection, as something which stood between him and the fruition of his desires.

His affair with Vyvyan seemed to have crystallized all this within him, to make him think and act with a ruthlessness and lawlessness hitherto foreign to him.

From a booth in a corner drug store he telephoned her at her cheap hotel.

"Hello, darling!" he said. "How do you feel?"

"Not so hot," she answered wearily. She sounded as if she had just awakened.

"I'm kinda tired myself," he admitted. "But it was a great night, so what's the difference.... Listen, Vyv, don't forget that we got a date again tonight?"

"I'm s'posed to see Al tonight."

"To hell with Al!" Tony burst out angrily. "You're not seein' Al any more. Get that, baby. An' if he gets rough, I'll take care of him. I can gather up just as many gorillas for a battle as he can. So don't worry about him. Leave as early as you can tonight—he never gets around till late—and meet me at the same corner where we met last night. An' be there, baby, or there'll be hell to pay."

The rest of the day Tony spent in making an inventory of all his rackets or ways of making money, with a few calls putting into smooth running order those that he had neglected somewhat recently and with other calls starting brand-new ones which were not a bit popular with the unwilling customers but which were going to be profitable to him. From now on he could afford to be interested only in the most profitable ones because he had a hunch that Vyvyan was going to be a mighty expensive proposition.

Lounging early that evening in his usual poolroom hang-out, Tony looked up in surprise as an ugly man slunk into the next chair and nudged him.

"Well?" said Tony coldly.

"You're Tony Guarino, ain't you?"

"Yeah. What of it?"

"Just this. If you go out with Al Spingola's moll again, you won't last a week. An dat's from de boss himself."

"What do you mean?" demanded Tony, though he knew well enough.

"Don't be dumb. Dey'll find you in an alley some night wit' your t'roat cut."

"I'll take my chances with him and his gorillas," bluffed Tony, and laughed. "A gun's better'n a knife any time and I can shoot better'n any of 'em. So run along, sonny, and tell your whole damn gang to chew that on their back teeth."

Tony laughed outright at the expression of amazement on the henchman's ugly face, then with a sneering smile watched the fellow move away. In his side coat pocket that revolver still rested comfortably and reassuringly. It was amazing how much courage that weapon put into him. It bridged the difference between a David and a Goliath—it always does to a born gangster. Also that afternoon he had, arranged for a friend of his who was a good shot to trail him everywhere he went at night now, and be ready to shoot down from behind anybody who tried to get Tony in the same way.

Vyvyan was nervous and shivery when she arrived at the appointed corner in a taxi and climbed into the roadster beside him.

"I'm scared, Tony," she said and gripped his arm while she looked back over her shoulder. Then she half screamed. "Oh, there's another car starting up after us,"

"Don't worry; that's my bodyguard."

"Oh!... Well, just as I started into the theater tonight the meanest looking man I ever saw stepped right in front of me and jammed a note into my hand. I wouldn't have been surprised if he had started to murder me right there. But he went on. When I got into my dressing room I read what he had given me. It was written in pencil, all scrawled and dirty, but plain enough. This is what it said: 'If you stand me up again, your life won't be worth a lead nickel. Remember that!' It was from Al, of course," she finished.

"Yeah. Another one o' his muggs tried to bluff me at the poolroom tonight but I told him I was able to take care of myself with Spingola or anybody else."

They drove to the same restaurant as the night before and were shown to the same little private dining room. Half an hour later the door was thrust open violently and Al Spingola stood framed in the opening. His swarthy face was a sort of ghastly gray, his eyes blazed with the fires of hell, and his brutal mouth was set in a nasty snarl. Most important of all, his right hand was plunged deep into his side coat pocket.

Tony had turned a strange greenish white and his eyes were glazed. The encounter between himself and Spingola had come at last and that it was a life-and-death fight was obvious.

"Al!" gasped Vyvyan. "Don't do—" Her voice trailed off.

Tony and Spingola were staring straight into each other's eyes. The younger man looked nervous; it isn't easy to kill your first man.

"So you couldn't take a warning, eh, you two punks; you thought you could get away with giving *me* the run-around."

"Who are you?" asked Tony, knowing that to be the most disconcerting thing he could say.

"Who'm I?" spluttered Spingola. "I'll show you—

And at that instant Tony fired through his coat pocket. He had been reaching for his napkin when Spingola came in. Immediately but without perceptible movement, his hand had shifted to his gun. He had had the drop on Spingola the whole time and had merely created a little diversion to make absolutely sure of winning his first gun battle.

Spingola looked surprised, then sagged to the floor. With a handkerchief Tony quickly rubbed his gun free of fingerprints, then threw the weapon out the window into the alley below.

"Come, dear," he said coldly, reaching for the shaking Vyvyan's arm. Now, that the deed was over, he felt strangely calm and strong, ready for anything.

He dropped a fifty-dollar bill on the table and rushed the girl down the back stairs. Through the alley they hurried, to where their roadster was parked. They raced away down an impenetrably dark street just as two uniformed policemen hurried in through the cafe's front door. Tony wasn't worried. He knew that the owner and waiters would give a description of the people who had occupied that private dining room but it would be so vague, in case it were not actually false, that it would be absolutely valueless to the police.

chapter 3

The killing of Al Spingola created a sensation. It happened just before America entered the World War, long before gangdom had achieved anything like its present power or affluence or willingness to murder in unique fashion. Fights were plentiful, of course, and an occasional stabbing did not arouse great excitement but actual gunplay was rare. Spingola had been about the first of the city's gang leaders to enforce his power with a gun and his being dropped off so suddenly was most disconcerting to the other leaders who had been about ready to use the same methods. But now they couldn't decide whether a gun was the best source of power or not.

The morning after the affray, Tony rose early, feeling a little rocky, and immediately induced his mother to sew the small burned hole in his coat, explaining that he had done it with a cigarette. Then he wisely decided not to wear that suit on the street again.

He went first to Klondike O'Hara's saloon. Klondike himself was behind the bar. A burly, red-faced young Irishman, he cut quite a dash in his own neighborhood as a gang leader and had been one of Spingola's most faithful enemies.

"I'm Tony Guarino," announced the boy, "from over on Taylor Street."

"Yeah?"

"I s'pose you read about Al Spingola gettin' his last night."

"Yeah," assented O'Hara cautiously, chewing on a black cigar.

"Well, I know you and him were enemies so I thought if they took me up for his death you'd see that I had a good lawyer and so on."

"You? Did you get that rat—a punk like you?"

"I didn't say so," retorted Tony doggedly. "I just wanted to know if they picked me up if you'd get me a lawyer."

"Betcher life. An' from now on you're welcome around here any time. I can always use another kid with guts."

"Thanks."

From O'Hara's saloon, Tony went to see Vyvyan at her cheap little hotel. She was nervous and tearful but back of the nervousness he could detect a new attitude of overbearing hardness, and behind the tears her green eyes held a glitter that did not reassure him. He wondered if she knew how much her silence meant to him —and decided that she probably did.

"You've taken Al away from me," she sobbed. "So now you'll have to take care of me the way he did."

"Shut up!" snapped Tony. "I'm going to. Let's rent a nice little flat today."

Thus within the space of twenty-four hours, Tony Guarino killed his first man, joined a regular gang and took unto himself a common law wife. Events move rapidly in underworld neighborhoods.

Tony didn't intend to move away from home himself just yet; it wouldn't look right to his folks.

Again he crossed the deadline between the domains governed by the Irish and those governed by the Italians, and started for O'Hara's saloon. A heavy car drew up to the curb and stopped with a screeching of brakes.

"Hey, kid!" shouted a raucous voice. "C'mere."

Tony's first impulse was to run, but having recognized the car as one of those from the Detective Bureau, he realized that to do so would mean being shot. So he walked over to them.

"Get in!" commanded a burly brute.

He practically dragged Tony into the tonneau and the car raced away. Arrived at the bureau, the whole party, with Ton/in the center, ascended to one of the conference rooms on the second floor.

"I s'pose you heard about Al Spingola bein' bumped off last night," said the man who appeared to be the leader of the party.

"Yes," assented Tony, not to be outdone. "I read it in the morning paper."

The half dozen men laughed nastily.

"The hell you did!" said the first one. "You knew all about it a long time before that. *Because you killed Al Spingola.*"

"Has the heat gone to your head?" demanded Tony coolly.

"Don't try to stall or it'll go hard with you. We know all about it. C'mon now and spill it."

"I don't know what you're talking about," retorted Tony as *if* greatly bored by the proceedings.

"Oh, you're goin' to be tough, eh?"

"No. Just truthful."

"Where were you last night from twelve to three o'clock?"

"Home in bed."

"Can you prove it?"

"My whole family would swear to it."

"Where'd you get *that?*" demanded another detective suddenly, and thrust before Tony's astonished eyes the revolver with which the Spingola killing had been committed.

The boy gulped but with a terrific effort retained his outward calm.

"I never saw it before," he retorted doggedly. He wondered just how much they did know. It looked bad. For those were the days when the police took the same interest in a gang killing as in any other murder and made, just as eager and earnest an effort to solve it. Well, the only thing to do was bluff it out.

"I never saw it before," he repeated, straightening up defiantly.

The leader of the party suddenly struck him a hard backhand slap across the mouth.

"Quit stallin'," he snarled. "C'mon an' tell us the truth."

"Cut the rough stuff!" snapped Tony coldly but his eyes were blazing. "I've got a brother that's a cop and I know all about the way you do people. Furthermore, I got a lot of powerful friends and I'm goin' to be a big shot in this town myself some day. So treat me decent an' it'll be better for all of us."

"Well, would you listen to that?" jeered one, of the dicks. "Of all the big-mouthed punks I ever seen—"

"I hear you been goin' around with one of Spingola's girls," said the leader.

Tony smiled. "From all I've heard, he had so many that half the girls in town were his."

"Naw, I mean his particular steady girl—his moll. You know the one I mean—that tall, spindly-legged blonde down at the Gaiety Theatre."

"Don't know her."

"There's been talk about you an' her goin' around among the wise-guys in your neighborhood the last two, three days. Everybody's been lookin' for trouble over it. An' now Al's dead."

"Well, that don't prove nothin' against me," argued Tony. "Even if all you say was true, it would be him that had a motive for bumpin' me off. And anyway, do you think as good a gunman as Spingola would ever let a kid like me get the drop on him?"

"T'ain't likely," admitted the leader of the squad.

There was a sudden commotion outside the door and a bright-eyed, bewhiskered little man came bustling into the room.

"I have here a writ of habeas corpus for the release of Mr. Tony Guarino," he announced with dignity and flourished a document.

The detectives gasped. For a writ to be run so soon indicated that the prisoner had connections. They had never dreamed that this kid was hooked up with the systematized elements of the underworld. But here the writ was. As they hadn't sufficient evidence to place a charge against Tony and book him, they had to honor the writ and release him.

"No hard feelings, boys," he said pleasantly as he followed the lawyer out.

chapter 4

Tony found his connection with the O'Hara gang active and pleasant. At first the Irish boys were somewhat suspicious of an Italian in their midst but when it was whispered around that it was he who had shot the redoubtable Al Spingola, their hostility vanished like fog in sunshine and they welcomed him with open enthusiasm. Tony himself never mentioned the occurrence, neither denying it nor bragging about it. But day and night he was watching for a reprisal from some of Spingola's henchmen. He still had his armed bodyguard following behind every time he went outside and not even the members of his own gang knew that.

Tony's executive ability soon revealed itself and before long he was acting as O'Hara's lieutenant. He made it plain to Klondike from the first, however, that he would not take a hand in second-story jobs, robberies, hold-ups or burglaries of any sort. And he explained his stand with his little phrase which later was to become so famous:

"I ain't riskin' a pinch for a coupla bucks."

It wasn't a matter of ethics with him; it was a matter of economics, the balancing of probable gain against probable risk and finding-out whether it was worth it. Anyway, there was no fun to rough stuff, no adventure or sportsmanship about it. Tony liked the smoother and wittier forms of larceny, those that bordered on extortion and blackmail. For instance, he could convince a small storekeeper in a few minutes that five or ten dollars a month was very cheap protection against having his store robbed or himself knocked on the head when he went home at night. And there were any amount of ignorant, fearful mothers who could be convinced readily that a quarter or half dollar per month per child was cheap insurance against having their children kidnapped and held for ransom. And once convinced, they paid their tribute regularly and unwhimperingly whenever he sent his collector around, just as they would insurance. He could think up two or three new schemes like that a day, and they always worked. As he said to O'Hara:

"What's the use of stickin' people up or bangin' 'em on the head when you can talk 'em out of it? My way's not only a lot safer but more fun."

On all sides now he was accorded the greatest respect. And he knew why; it was because the word had gone around that he was a killer. He had killed only once, really in self-defense, and actuated largely by fear, yet he was marked as a killer and through life he would be subject to the advantages and disadvantages that went with the appellation.

His income now was running about three hundred a week—which was enormous for a gangster before Prohibition came along and made them millionaires—and with Vyvyan's help he was managing to have a nice time. He had taken a nicer flat for her by now and she had quit the show.

"I just can't bear to think of other men starin' at them pretty legs of yours, kid," he explained when insisting that she quit. "I'm makin' plenty o' dough for both of us, so throw up the job."

Being fond, like most blondes, of an easy life secured with the smallest possible expenditure of energy, she obeyed orders. Tony himself was still living at home but intended to move as soon as he could get up the necessary courage. His brother Ben, the police-man, hearing of his headquarters grilling over the Spingola killing, had given him another one at home while the rest of the family wailed in the background. But the wily Tony had been grimly silent at the right moments and suavely voluble at others, with the result that he convinced his family, just as he had the detectives, that he had nothing to do with Spingola's demise.

Tony went to Vyvyan's flat shortly before seven one Saturday night, feeling in rather high spirits.

"Well, kid, what do you want to do tonight?" he asked.

"Let's go to Colosimo's."

"Naw, I don't like that joint. Let's go out to one of those nice North Side places."

"*No,* I want to go to Colosimo's." Her lower lip puckered threat-eningly.

"Naw, I don't like that joint, I said."

"Why not?"

"A lot of the old Spingola mob do their stepping out there on Saturday night."

"Afraid?" she sneered. She seemed to be in a nasty humor tonight.

"No!" he snapped. "But I never liked the idea of bein' shot in the back."

"Oh, all right, if that's the way you feel about it. How about Ike Bloom's?"

"Well, it ain't very far from Colosimo's, but it has a lot nicer peo-ple. All right, we'll go there if you wanta."

Tony kept most of his wardrobe at the flat. He bathed and shaved now, and dressed carefully in a well-tailored, nicely pressed tuxe-do. But when he stepped out into the living room, there was a revolver in a shoulder holster hanging in his left armpit, and a tiny blue steel automatic fitted snugly into his right vest pocket.

Vyvyan was quite stunning in a flashing green evening gown and a soft white cloak. They made a handsome couple as they descend-ed to the street and entered the waiting limousine. It belonged to

Tony; he had made good his promise of having a car better than his brother's and of getting it as easily.

At Ike Bloom's enormous and beautiful cabaret on Twenty-second Street, they took a table at the edge of the balcony, a point of vantage from which they could see everything without being at all conspicuous themselves. And they were around at one end of the horseshoe-shaped cafe, so that Tony might have his back to the wall and therefore enjoy the evening more.

They had a splendid dinner, with excellent champagne, saw the sparkling if somewhat naked revue, then relaxed—smoking, drinking, chatting—until the evening's gaiety began shortly after eleven. Tony scrutinized carefully the other guests as they entered. But by twelve-thirty, when the place was practically filled, he hadn't seen an enemy, nor even anyone of whom he was suspicious. So he consented to dance with Vyvyan.

They took advantage of almost every dance after that, drinking and nibbling at various inconsequential but expensive items of food between times. And every hour a new revue was presented.

During the presentation of one of these shows, while a huge woman with a nice voice and too many diamonds, crooned something about lovin' in the moonlight, Tony suddenly sat straight up, his gaze riveted to a woman straight across from him at the other end of the balcony. She was a brunette, a stunning brunette, obviously young, and dressed in a gorgeous white evening gown. The bulky young man with her looked like a prizefighter.

"What a dame!" breathed Tony in admiration.

"Where?" snapped Vyvyan.

"That brunette over there in white."

Vyvyan looked, anxiously and with narrowed gaze. Then she glanced back at Tony.

"I can't imagine what you see in her," she snapped scornfully.

"Jealous?"

"Of that? I should say not. And that bum with her looks like a burglar."

"Maybe he is," assented Tony imperturbably. "There's worse professions. But she's a stunner. I wonder who she is."

"Some common hussy, I'll bet."

"Well, I'll bet she ain't," snapped Tony, and Beckoned the waiter over. "Say, do you know who that dame is—the good-lookin' brunette in white over there?"

The waiter looked, then smiled.

"That's Miss Jane Conley," he answered.

"Never heard that dame before," muttered Tony.

"Perhaps you've heard of her under her other name," suggested the waiter. "She's known mostly as 'The Gun Girl.'"

"My God!" gasped Tony. "Is *she* the gun girl?"

"Yes, sir. Though we like to keep it quiet because we don't want any trouble here."

"No, of course not," agreed Tony drily.

"Who's the gun girl?" demanded Vyvyan snappishly when the waiter had gone.

"Well, kid, I'll wise you up a little on underworld stuff, though God knows that ain't the only thing you're dumb in. A really good gunman is usually pretty well known, not only to other crooks but to the cops. Whenever they see him on the street, they stop him and frisk him, to see if he's up to something. He can't go two blocks in any direction without bein' stopped and frisked by somebody—either dicks or harness bulls. So he has to have somebody else—usually a good-lookin' well-dressed girl that nobody would suspect—carry his gat for him and trail him till he's ready to use it. Then she hurries up, slips it to him and strolls slowly down the block. He pulls off his job and runs down the street, slippin' her the gat as he goes past. Immediately she disappears—street-car, taxi, or afoot, any way—but without lookin' like she's in a hurry. So if he should git pinched, they, can't find anything on him. See?"

"I don't see anything so grand in that."

"You don't, eh? Well, let me tell you, there's nothin' scarcer than a good gun girl. It takes brains and a lot of guts. That girl across there—if that waiter didn't lie to me—is the most famous of all of 'em. She's known as *The* Gun Girl. I've heard about her for a couple years but I didn't even know what her name was. She started out in New York, workin' with Leech Benson.

When he finally got sent up she switched over to Lefty Kelly and when he got killed she come out here to work for Ace Darby. I guess she's still workin' for him. I wonder if that's him with her now."

"No, it isn't."

"How do you know?"

"Because I met him one time—at a party."

They went down to dance again. The Gun Girl and her escort also were dancing. And the fascinated Tony, finding the girl even more beautiful and charming at close range, kept his glance on her so much that it was some time before he realized that a man was trying to flirt with Vyvyan. A large, bulky man dressed in a gray business suit that fitted him none too well, a man who looked old enough to know better. He was dancing with a tiny blonde that he folded up in his arms as a child would a doll. Evidently he had a weakness for blondes. But he was no gentleman. He was obviously drunk and making a show of himself.

He waved at Vyvyan and winked portentously as the two couples came near each other for an instant. Tony's swarthy complexion began turning a sort of deep purple. The next time the two couples converged, the man spoke:

"Hello, cutie!" he exclaimed with a grin. "How about the next dance?"

Tony released his partner, snatched the little blonde out of the big man's arms and clouted the man solidly on the jaw, a blow so hard that it not only knocked the man down but slid him ten feet along the dance floor.

"Come *on,* kid, let's get out of this," snapped Tony and grabbed Vyvyan's wrist.

There was a small, seldom-used stairway that led up almost directly to their table. They hurried up and Tony beckoned frantically to the waiter.

That was a grand sock you gave him, sir," smiled the waiter as he quickly added up the check. "And he sure had it comin' to him. But there's sure to be an awful row when becomes to. You know who he is, don't you?"

"No."

"Captain Flanagan."

"Oh, my God!"

Tony glanced at the check, then threw down a fifty-dollar bill and rushed Vyvyan out of the place.

"Who's Captain Flanagan?" asked the girl as they raced away.

"Chief of Detectives, and supposed to be the hardest-boiled man on the force."

"Do you suppose you'll have any trouble over this?"

"Well, it won't do me any *good,"* retorted Tony grimly. '

Four blocks away he slowed down to allow his rear guard to catch up to within half a block. Then when he saw the other car's headlights reflected in his side mirror he increased his speed again.

They drew up in front of Vyvyan's flat and she climbed out quickly. Then a car rushed past, spouting fire and bullets, and whizzed away into the night. Vyvyan screamed and turned back.

"Tony!" she called. "Are you hurt?"

He crawled up from the floor where he cautiously had thrown himself the moment he heard the high-pitched song of the other machine's racing motor.

"No, they didn't touch me!" he growled. "But it wasn't their fault. Lucky you were out of the car because there wouldn'ta been room for two on the floor.... Say, you got out in an awful hurry. Did you know anything about the arrangements for this little party?"

"Why, Tony, how can you say such a thing?"

"A man can say a lot of things when somebody's just tried to kill him."

chapter 5

Captain Flanagan showed his teeth immediately. Monday noon a squad of detectives from the bureau burst into Klondike O'Hara's saloon, singled Tony out from the crowd lounging about and ordered him to come along.

"I know what this is all about," said Tony to the bewildered and apprehensive O'Hara. "And I think it'll come out all right. Anyway, wait a coupla hours before sending down a mouthpiece with a writ."

They took Tony straight to the detective bureau and ushered him roughly into Captain Flanagan's office, then slammed the door, leaving the two men alone. Flanagan rose and came around from behind his desk. He was a big man, broad and thick, with a belligerent jaw, a nasty sneering mouth and gimlet-like, bloodshot gray eyes that were set too close together.

"So you're the hoodlum that socked me at Ike Bloom's the other night, eh?" he snarled.

"Yes, sir," said Tony calmly. "And anybody else would have done the same. You would have yourself if somebody kept insulting the girl you were with."

"Is that so? Well, I don't imagine a hood like you would have a dame with him that *could* be insulted. So there!"

Without warning, he gave Tony a terrific backhand slap across the mouth, a hard stinging blow that staggered the boy for a moment and made him draw in his breath sharply as he became conscious of the pain in his bruised lips. Then his eyes glinted with fury and his hands went up.

"Don't lift your hands to me, you punk!" snarled Flanagan. "Or I'll call in a dozen men from out there and have 'em beat you half to death with rubber hoses."

"You would," assented Tony bitterly. "You're the type."

"What do you mean—I'm the type?"

"Nothin'."

"What's your game, anyhow?"

"I haven't any."

"No? Well, you hang around with Klondike O'Hara's mob, and they're a bunch of bad eggs. Come on now, quit stallin'—what's your racket?"

"Nothing—in particular."

"Well, what do you do for O'Hara?"

"Obey orders."

"Oh, a smart guy, eh?" sneered Flanagan. He slapped Tony again, then reached for his hip as the boy automatically lifted his hands. "Put down your hands, you thug. I'll teach you to have some respect for your betters. Come on now, what's your game—second-story, stick-up or what?"

"I never was in on a stick-up or any other kind of a rough job in my life," retorted Tony proudly.

"Well, just how do you get all these good clothes and the big car I understand you own?"

"I got ways of my own."

"I don't doubt it," agreed Flanagan with dry sarcasm. "That's what I want to know about—these ways of yours. Come on now and talk, or I'll have the boys give you a pounding you'll never forget."

"I wouldn't if I were you," answered Tony, his eyes and tone coldly menacing. "I might be a big shot in this town yet—and payin' you off."

"What do you mean—payin' me off?" snarled Flanagan. "Do you mean to say that I could be bought?"

"I don't see why not—all the other dicks can. You'd be an awful fool not to get yours while you could."

"Of all the impudent punks!" gasped the chief of detectives. His rage was so great that he seemed to be swelling out of his collar. "Listen here, you," he said

finally. "I ain't got any more time to waste on you. But I'm givin' you just twenty-four hours to get out of town. And you better go. Get me?"

"Yeah. But that don't mean I'm goin'." And the boy strode out of the office.

Tony went back to O'Hara's saloon with cut lips and murder in his heart, and explained the whole thing to Klondike himself. The gang leader was obviously upset.

"It's bad business, kid," he said slowly. "Flanagan's hard-boiled and he can make life miserable for anybody if he wants to."

"To hell with him!" scoffed Tony. "He ain't so much."

Tony remained in town beyond his allotted time. And he soon discovered that Klondike O'Hara was right. For he found himself involved in a police persecution more complete than he had thought possible. He was halted half a dozen times a day, in O'Hara's place, on the street, anywhere and everywhere, stopped and searched and questioned. He dare not carry a gun because if they found him with one he knew they'd give him the works; yet he knew that the remains of the Spingola gang were actively and murderously oh his trail. It was a nerve-racking week.

The detectives even burst into Vyvyan's flat one night when he was there and turned the place upside down on the pretext of looking for stolen property. And they questioned her with more thoroughness than gallantry.

"So that's the dame you swiped from Al Spingola?" said one of them to Tony with a leer in Vyvyan's direction. "Well, I don't blame him for gettin' mad. She sure ain't hard to look at.... How about a little date some night, kid?"

"Listen—" began Tony ominously.

"I don't even speak to dicks if I can help it," retorted Vyvyan and turned away with her nose in the air.

"Well, there's probably been a good many times in your life When you couldn't help it," snapped the detective. "And there's goin' to be a lot more if you keep hangin' around with the likes of this gorilla. So don't high-hat us, baby; we might be able to give you a break sometime."

On Friday Klondike O'Hara called Tony into the office, a cluttered frowsy little room with a battered roll-top desk and two once golden oak chairs. The Irishman was coatless and his spotted, unbuttoned vest flapped unconfined save for such restraint as his heavy gold watch chain strung across its front placed upon it. His derby was pushed forward over his eyes until its front almost rested on the bridge of his nose, and a thoroughly chewed, unlighted cigar occupied one corner of his slit-like, tobacco-stained mouth.

"Sit down, Tony," he invited.

Tony sat, feeling very uncomfortable and wondering what this portended. Ordinarily O'Hara gave orders, received reports and loot, and conducted all the other business of his gang over one end of the bar. When he held a conference in the office, it was something important.

"I been worried all week," began the leader, "about you. The dicks are after you, kid; there's no doubt about it. And because of that Flanagan business, they're going to keep after you till they get you. Flanagan's hard-boiled and he hangs on like a bulldog—when he wants to. If you was big enough to pass him a heavy piece of change every week he'd prob'ly lay off. But you ain't. So you got to take it. In the meantime this is goin' to get me and the whole mob in dutch at headquarters. Those dicks that come pokin' around here every day are after you, of course, but just the same they've got an eye out for anything else they can see. If they keep that up long enough they're bound to see or hear somep'n that'll ruin us. So I'm goin' to have to ask you not to come around here."

"So you're givin' me the gate, eh?" demanded Tony coldly.

"Not that. Jeez, kid, I like you and I'd like to have you with me always. But don't you see that bein' under the police spotlight this way is sure to ruin us?"

"Yes, I guess maybe you're right. But what about the ideas I give you, the schemes I started?"

"You'll keep gettin' your cut on 'em every week; I'll send it every Saturday night any place you say. And I'll play square with you, kid; I want you to have everything that's comin' to you. But I just don't dare let you stick around here; it wouldn't be fair to the rest of the boys."

They shook hands and Tony walked out, dismissed because of the unwelcome attention that his persecution by the police was bringing down upon the whole gang.

In the bar, one of the O'Hara henchmen sidled up to him.

"Listen," he said out of one corner of his mouth, "I heard today that the Spingola mob's out to get you."

"They've tried it before," retorted Tony coldly.

"I know. But this time it's for blood; they say they're not goin' to miss."

"Thanks," said Tony. "Well, I guess I'll have to go back to packin' a gun, dicks or no dicks, and take a chance on bein' able to throw it away if they pick me up."

Tony moved slowly out to the sidewalk and beckoned his bodyguard, who was lounging in a doorway across the street, smoking a cigarette. The boy came across the street, a slender, white-faced chap with a weak chin and burning black eyes.

"I just got a tip that the Spingola mob's after me right," said Tony. "And I ain't got a gun. I'm goin' to the flat now to get my artillery. So watch sharp."

He glanced quickly up and down the street then he timed and started down the sidewalk, walking briskly, his keen glance roving suspiciously in all directions, the other boy trailing along some thirty yards behind, his hand plunged deep into his right coat pocket.

Vyvyan was beginning to grow restive under the strain of this constant surveillance and heckling by the police. She was wrought up and irritable at dinner and Tony went out to a movie alone.

America had entered the World War but a few days before and the screen flashed an appeal for volunteers to join the army for immediate overseas service. Tony wondered what sort of saps would fall for that. Not he. What did he owe the country? What had the country ever done for him? He was chuckling cynically to himself as he walked out at the conclusion of the show.

His glance roved over the crowd, seeking possible enemies, either those of the law or those outside it. But he saw none and started home, walking briskly, for his car was not yet out of the garage where he had placed it for repairs following the attempt on his life in front of Vyvyan's flat the Saturday night before.

Turning off the business thoroughfare of the district and plunging deeper into the dark, deserted side streets, Tony suddenly became aware of other footfalls besides his own. Turning his head cautiously, he saw three men across the street but a little to the rear, and walking in the same direction as himself. Something seemed to grow cold within him and his hand quietly sought the ready gun in his side coat pocket.

But first he must test his Belief that these men were after him— that they were killers from the Spingola mob. At the next corner he turned to the left and increased his pace. Quickly the other men crossed the street and followed, half-running until they were again in their preferred position across the street from him and slightly to the rear.

Tony realized that their task of the night was to assassinate him, that they were only waiting until he reached some prearranged or some favorite spot of theirs. And there was no possible way of escaping their murderous attentions. To run would only hasten their fire; to shout would accomplish the same end and no one would come to his assistance, for minding one's own business had been developed to a fine art in this neighborhood. There was nothing to do but wait and shoot it out with them when they opened the attack.

The horror of his situation, of being trailed to his death with almost the same inevitability as a legal execution, never struck him, for, like all gangsters, Tony was totally without imagination.

The men suddenly swerved and began crossing the street, moving toward a position directly behind him. Knowing the tremendous value of a surprise attack, Tony decided to pull one. With the swift-ness of a shadow, he faded into a doorway and began firing. The guns of the three men answered viciously and bullets thudded and whined about the boy. From beyond he could see the flashes and hear the reports of his bodyguard's gun. The assassins were between two fires.

Tony himself, partly sheltered and cold as ice, was firing slowly but with deadly effect. He saw one of the men go down and stay down. He saw another go down for a moment, then scramble to his feet and flee, limping, with the third. The enemy had been routed.

In the distance he heard the peculiar "Clang-clang-clang!" of a detective bureau squad car. Undoubtedly they had heard the shots and now were racing there. Tony dodged out of the sheltering door-way and hurried past the inert figure without pausing to glance at it. Catching up with his bodyguard, he led him into a dark, smelly alley at a run.

"Good work, kid!" panted Tony as they ran and slipped the boy a twenty-dollar bill. "We bumped off one and winged another. But we got to cover our tracks fast and complete. Throw your gun over one of these fences." His own went over and the other boy's followed. "Now, if we're pinched, there's nothin' on us. But we don't want to get pinched. At the end of the alley we split. Get as far from here as you can as quick as possible but don't move so fast that you'll attract attention. If you should be picked up, you haven't seen me all evening. You been to a movie. See?"

The boy nodded and as they reached the end of the alley on another street, swerved to the right and disappeared in the darkness. Tony turned to the left. Within five minutes he was seven blocks away from the scene of the shooting. In that hurried walk, he had done a lot *of* thinking. Undoubtedly that dead man was a member of the Spingola mob. The police who found him would know that, of course, and they would have a pretty good idea as to how he came to his death. Tony realized that they would begin looking for him immediately. Between the police and the Spingola mob— for tonight's occurrence would only increase their thirst for his blood—the town was going to be too hot to hold him for a while. He would have to leave for a few months. But where could he go? What could he do? Then he remembered that appeal on the movie screen tonight. And he chuckled. He would join the army. It had a lot of advantages, now that he began to catalogue them—nobody would ever think of looking for him there, he'd do some traveling and see a lot of new things at no expense to himself, and so on. The war wouldn't last long, now that America was in it; he'd have a nice vacation for a few months.

In the meantime, his predicament was serious. The police were sure to be looking for him immediately in all his known haunts. He dare not go home, nor to Vyvyan's, nor to O'Hara's place. He went into a drug store and telephoned O'Hara.

"Hello, Klon," he said in a guarded tone. "This is Tony. I just had a battle with some of the Spingola mob. Bumped off one and nicked another. I s'pose the dicks'll be lookin' for me right away. I've decided to get out of town for a while. And I want to see you and Vyvyan before I go, but I don't dare come either to your place nor to hers. Where can we meet?"

"Better meet at the flat of one of my dames, I guess," answered O'Hara. He gave the name and address. "We ought to be safe there. I'll hurry right over there and be waiting for you."

Tony telephoned Vyvyan, then hailed a cab. The address proved to be a large apartment house in a quiet section. Ascertaining that the flat he wanted was on the third floor, Tony hurried up and knocked quietly.

O'Hara admitted him and introduced him to a large horsy blonde named Gertie. Gertie had lots of yellow hair, pale, empty-looking blue eyes with dark circles of dissipation under them, and an ample figure wrapped in a lavender negligee with quantities of dyed fur. She wore lavender mules with enormous pompoms but her legs were bare. She laughed loudly and hollowly on the slightest pretext and seemed to have a consuming fear that everybody wouldn't get enough to drink. The apartment was a rococo affair done in French style, with the walls hung in blue taffeta, and jammed so full of ornate furniture that one could hardly walk.

Tony quickly explained the situation and his plan of getting away for a while. O'Hara approved it and promised to send Vyvyan and Mrs. Guarino money every week, Tony's share of the profits from the rackets he had conceived and instituted.

Then Vyvyan arrived and O'Hara, with a penetration rare in one of his type, led Gertie out into another room so that Tony could be alone with Vyvyan for a few moments. Quickly he explained everything to her, then told her of his resolve to join the army.

"But you might be killed," she objected.

Tony grinned. "Well, if I stay here, I'm either goin' to get bumped off or be sent away for a few years."

"But, Tony, I can't do without you," sniffed Vyvyan.

"I've arranged with O'Hara to send you money every week," answered the boy shrewdly. "So you'll manage to get along for a few months—till I get back. Oh, I'm comin' back—don't worry about that. And when I get back," he said with an ominous edge in his voice, "I'll expect you to be waitin' for me."

"I will, Tony, oh, I will." She was clinging to him now, kissing him with great fervor and sobbing furiously. "Oh, I love you so, kid. Please come back to me."

He kissed her with all the passion that had made him risk his life to get her, that had made him kill for her, then hurried out with O'Hara, her sobs and pleas for his return ringing in his ears. O'Hara drove him to South Bend, Tony lying down in the tonneau of the car until they were beyond the city limits. There was a New York train that came through there shortly after one in the morning. Tony caught it. Two days later he was in the army, and lost from all his enemies. They didn't ask many questions of men who wanted to be a soldier then.

chapter 6

Tony Guarino made a good soldier. They put him into a machine gun company and he loved it. Officers considered his nerveless coolness under fire remarkable. They didn't know that being under fire was an old story to him, and that he was unaccustomed to having countless thousands of men to help him repel the attack. Trenches, too, were a protection unknown in the street battles back home. All in all, he considered war a rather tame proposition and plunged into it with gusto.

Within six months he was first sergeant of his company. The men, being mostly country boys and therefore having nothing in common with him, didn't like him very well personally but he had that indefinable "it" of the born leader that would have made them unquestionably follow him anywhere. They had to, once. It was a nasty night engagement in the woods. Tony came staggering out of the dark, carrying the unconscious captain on his back, and almost blinded by his own blood, to find all their officers down and the leaderless men on the verge of panic. Tony let the captain Carefully to the ground, instructed two men to do what they could for him from their first-aid kits, then dashed the blood out of his eyes and quietly took command of the situation.

Shortly after dawn the amazed colonel discovered Tony in command of three companies, with his position well consolidated and holding his section of the line comfortably. Tony himself was sitting on a little hillock, in deadly peril from snipers, with his automatic lying on his knee and with his keen glance wandering up and down the line in an effort to find some man who seemed disposed to retreat. He was somewhat of a sight, with his legs bare and muddy, and his head tied up in bloody handkerchiefs and his puttees; only his eyes and mouth remained uncovered.

"Of all the dashed impudence!" exclaimed the colonel to the officers with him. "Taking command of the whole works and running it better than many a major could have done. If the Heinies had penetrated through here, they'd have wiped us out. Say," he called to Tony from the shelter of the messy trench through which he was making his way in an effort to gather up his scattered regiment, "come down from there and go back and have your wounds dressed."

"We ain't got any officers," retorted Tony doggedly. "Most of 'em got bumped off during the night but a few only got nicked and I sent them back to get patched up. They wouldn'ta gone, of course, if they'd been conscious but they was all out like a light so I didn't have any trouble with 'em. The men fight grand when there's somebody to see to 'em," he continued, "but they're a little skittish when there ain't. So I'm seein' to 'em till some officers get here."

"Damme!" exclaimed the colonel to his staff. "Can you beat that; argues with me to stay up there and get his head blown off?" Then he raised his voice and called to Tony again: "I'm Colonel Riley. I'll have Captain Stone here to see to your men. Now you come down from there—*at once,* do you hear?—and go back and have your wounds dressed. I can't afford to have a man like you getting infection and dying on me."

So Tony scrambled down from his dangerous observatory hillock, saluted the colonel, who silently shook hands with him, and reluctantly started for the rear.

Before the day was over, Colonel Riley was in possession of a complete story of the night's activities and he sent a report into G.H.Q. that would have made Tony's ears ring. They gave Tony the D.S.C. and the Croix de Guerre for that night's work and he couldn't see what for; he'd merely done what the situation demanded, the same as he would in a street fight back home.

Eventually came the Armistice and Tony was sent home. He was ready to go home. Being a shrewd gambler he had taken the saps for a ride, running his small capital up to something over six thousand dollars, which he carried in cash in a belt around his waist under his tunic. And there had been many a time in France when he would have given all of it for an hour with Vyvyan.

Having perfected him in every branch of the fine art of murder and having made every effort to readjust his mental processes so that he was willing at any time to translate this knowledge and technique into action, the government, in turning him loose with its blessing in the shape of an honorable discharge, seemed to expect him to forget it all immediately and thereafter be a peaceable, law-abiding citizen. Which was a lot to ask of any man, much less Tony.

He had come home with a new face and a lot of new ideas, ideas that were going to be profitable for him but detrimental to the community in which he put them into practice. That awful night battle in the woods which had gained him the medals—he had them buttoned up in an inside pocket, not even showing the ribbons where anybody could see them—had also left him with a long livid scar down the left side of his face, a heavy scar running from the top of his ear to the point of his chin. In some manner the nerves and muscles around his mouth had become involved in the matter and now the left corner of his mouth was drawn upward permanently, not much but it had changed his appearance surprisingly. When he smiled, that corner didn't, and it gave his face an amazingly sinister look.

He hurried eagerly out of the depot, looking boyish and jaunty in his uniform and overseas cap. He had a grip and in the side pocket of his tunic a German officer's automatic that he had brought home as a souvenir.

Now that he was home, the first thing was to see Vyvyan. God! wouldn't it be grand to have her in his arms again, to feel her lithe, supple body pliant and vibrant against his? He hailed a taxi and gave the address, ordering the driver to step on it. His hungry eyes recognized the building, even in the dark, two blocks away, and his glance sought their old apartment. Yes, there was a light. She was home! That is, if she still lived there. He added that as an afterthought, as a dreadful possibility. Then he grunted and grinned. Vyv would be waiting; he remembered how she had sobbed and promised that night he left.

He gave the driver a handsome tip for his speed and, hurrying inside, eagerly scanned the names beside the letter boxes. Yes, there it was in the same place— Vyvyan Lovejoy. What a surprise his coming would be to her; he hadn't written for two months, there'd been so much else to do. He tried the hall door on the chance that it might be open. It was. He hurried softly upstairs and with his breath catching in his throat knocked at the familiar third floor door. He heard a sort of scuffling sound inside but no one came. He knocked again, loud and a little impatiently.

Then the door opened slightly. Tony's ready arms dropped to his sides and his eyes suddenly flashed fire. For holding the door was a man, a ratty-looking young fellow with a crook's face but sensual lips and a passionate nose. He was in his shirtsleeves.

With a lunge, Tony flung the door wide open, almost overturning the other man as he did so, and plunged into the room.

"Where's Vyvyan?" he demanded.

She came hurrying out of the bedroom, wrapped in a beautiful negligee that he had bought her. He could see that she had on only pajamas beneath it and that her legs were bare.

"Who are you?" she demanded furiously. "And what do you mean by breaking in here this way?"

Tony caught his breath; she didn't recognize him.

"Why, I'm Tony. I know I've changed a little," his fingers unconsciously felt that awful scar on his left cheek, "but surely you—"

"Tony!" she exclaimed in amazement and came closer to stare wonderingly up into his face. "Why they reported you killed about six weeks ago; it was in the papers."

"Well, I wasn't. I'm right here, and as good as ever." Then he suddenly remembered that strange man, who had closed the door by now and was waiting behind him. He whirled, facing them both accusingly. "Who's that?" he demanded, and in his voice was a tone that made Vyvyan cringe.

"A—a friend of mine," she answered.

"A friend of yours, eh?" he repeated bitterly and stared contemptuously at the other.

He whirled and rushed back to the bedroom. There in the closet, all mixed up with Vyvyan's things, he found a man's shoes, half a dozen masculine suits, even a man's pajamas. His things had been there when he went to war; but they were all gone now—these things were strange, evidently the property of that rat-faced crook in the parlor. Tony rushed back there, trembling with fury.

"So you two-timed me, you little bitch!" he snarled through gritted teeth. "I s'pose you been feedin' *him* out o' the money I had Klondike O'Hara send you every week."

"No, Tony," gasped Vyvyan breathlessly. Her hands fluttered to her throat and she seemed to find it almost impossible to speak. "Tony, you mustn't think what you're thinkin'. I never looked at another man all the time you was gone, not until that report about you bein' killed; I swear to God I didn't."

"Well, you didn't wait long after; a woman don't go to livin' with a man the first night she meets him. You didn't take the trouble to find out if that report was true; you didn't wait for a little while to see if I might come back, like I did. No, you grabbed somep'm else right away. And I don't see any mourning among your clothes; they're all just as wild and gay as ever. A lot you cared about me, outside of a meal ticket." Suddenly he saw red; his mind seemed frozen with rage. Automatically his hand darted to that pistol in his pocket. "You didn't give a damn about me, you lousy little—"

The dreadful word he flung at her was drowned in the roar of the gun. She clutched at her throat and fell, a fluffy, blood-stained heap. The man had dodged and was trying to hide behind a chair. But Tony mowed him down with deadly precision. Then he secreted the empty pistol under the cushion of an overstuffed chair and hurried out of the apartment, still carrying his bag.

chapter 7

It was after midnight. He saw no one on his way out. He had seen no one on his way in. He felt sure he was safe from identifying witnesses.

Two blocks away he hailed a taxi and gave the driver the name of one of the best hotels in town. The police, even if they were looking for Tony Guarino, would never think of looking for him at a hotel like that.

There were many uniforms on the streets and even in the lobby of the rather expensive hotel to which he went. It was not a conspicuous costume. He registered as *I. H. Stevens, Denver, Colo.,* and was shown to a handsome room with private bath.

He removed his tunic and stretched out in an easy chair to smoke and think. He had killed Vyvyan and her new lover. There was no doubt of that; three or four shots from a Luger aimed with his skill would finish anybody. And he did not regret his act. Vyvyan never had loved him; he could see it now. In fact, he felt a sense of relief that her mouth was, shut forever. She could have turned him in for that Spingola killing any time she liked, and she Was just the type to do it if something made her jealous or mad. Yes, he could breathe easier now that she was gone.

So he had been reported killed, eh? He wondered if Vyvyan had been lying about that, if she had only used it as a subterfuge to try to justify her conduct. He must know; for the answer to that question would have a large part in shaping his future course of action.

He reached for the telephone at his elbow and called Klondike O'Hara's saloon.

"Lemme talk to Klondike," he said in a hoarse, disguised voice.

"Klondike was bumped off about six months ago," answered a strange voice.

"That's too bad. I been away for some time and I hadn't heard about it. What I wanted was to find out where I could reach a kid that used to work for Klondike—Tony Guarino, his name was."

"Him? Aw, he got patriotic and joined the army right after war was declared. And he was killed in France just a week or so before the Armistice."

"How do you know he was?"

"It was in the papers—in a list of killed and wounded. Say, who are you, anyway?"

But Tony had hung up. And in his eyes flamed a great elation. So it was true. Everybody here at home thought he was dead. No longer would the police or the Spingola mob be looking for Tony Guarino. That his appearance was changed even more than he realized was proven by the fact that even Vyvyan had not recognized him at first. His old identity was dead; he would let it stay dead and go on his way as a new man. That course would cause his family no suffering; they already had done, of course, the same grieving as if he really had been killed. He laughed aloud. What a break!

He arose late, after a good sleep, and went down to a large store adjoining the hotel, where he purchased a complete outfit of civilian clothes. Leaving instructions to have the packages delivered to his hotel room immediately, he returned to the hotel lobby, purchased the morning papers and ascended to his room.

He found the killing of Vyvyan and her lover featured prominently in all the papers. And it was played up as a deep mystery. He discovered from the articles that the man in the case was "Frog" Merlin, owner of a North Side gambling house and reputed bootlegger. The death weapon had not been found and there were no known clues to the perpetrator of the crime. Detective Sergeant Ben Guarino was in charge of the case.

Tony read that last line three times then laughed uproariously. So Ben was a detective sergeant now. Well! Well! Wouldn't it be funny if they met some time? Then Tony's face hardened. Perhaps it wouldn't be so funny.

When the packages arrived, Tony donned his new outfit, then descended to the street. After a hearty breakfast he went out to the old neighborhood. It was an almost irresistible temptation to rush to the little grocery store and see the family but he steeled himself and turned in the opposite direction. He saw many people that he knew but he gave no sign of recognition, and none of them even gave him a second glance.

He spent the day in various illicit barrooms, listening to everything he could hear, asking as many and as detailed questions as he dared. He found the situation about as he had expected. The booze traffic was making the gangsters wealthy, and already the competition over the enormous profits was beginning to become acrimonious. Killings were liable to commence any time.

One man had held complete control of the situation for some little time after Prohibition came in. Then he was killed by being thrown from his horse on the Lincoln Park bridle path—what a horribly prosaic death for a gangster, for a man who had lived violently and who had every right to expect to die the same way. All of his lieutenants had tried to succeed him but none had been strong enough to gain the support of a majority of the gang. So they had split, each taking those loyal to him, and now there were half a dozen main gangs spread over the city,, each holding sovereignty over a certain section and daring the others to trespass.

Tony could see that the big profits ultimately would go to the man with a well-oiled organization which was run as any other business enterprise. For he knew that the average gangster—even the leaders—had no more executive ability than the revolver with which he ruled. The only thing he knew was the old law of the survival of the fittest—might made right and the devil took the hindmost. But when you fought him with brains as well as strength, you had him licked.

Tony's, inquiries showed him that the best executive of the lot was Johnny Lovo, who had his headquarters in Cicero, a rather large but somewhat frowsy suburb which joined the city on the west. Though the stranger could not discern where the city left off and the suburb began, Cicero was a separate entity with its own government and the city police had no right to meddle there. It impressed Tony as an ideal place from which to operate and that night he went out to see Johnny Lovo.

Those were the days before the present great secrecy as to gang leaders' movements and whereabouts was necessary and Tony had no difficulty in locating his man at his headquarters on an upper floor of a hotel whose appearance was far better than its reputation.

Lovo was a short, squat, dark man of perhaps thirty-five, with fine clothes, a large diamond ring and stickpin, and a ready smile on his not unhandsome face, who constantly chewed a long black cigar. He had been prominent in Cicero for some years as an operator of vice and gambling dens. Prohibition had merely placed in his hands another weapon with which to continue his pursuit of enormous wealth.

Tony liked him instantly. Here was a man who not only could act and give orders but who could plan.

"I just got out of the army two days ago," explained Tony without preliminaries. "And I want to get in this racket. I'd like to join up with you."

"Yes? Who are you?" asked Lovo with the natural suspicion of his kind.

"Tony—Camonte." His former identity was dead; he intended to let it remain so.

"Ever been with any mob before?" Lovo's keen eyes were examining him thoroughly.

"Yes, sir. I was Klondike O'Hara's main lieutenant before the war. But of course I don't want that known now; I want to forget it."

"Don't blame you. That was small-time stuff."

"Not so small," defended Tony quickly. "My end used to run around three hundred a week."

"Really?" Lovo was viewing him with heightened interest. "You must have been clever."

"I was," admitted Tony frankly, then added proudly: "And I never pulled any rough stuff either, no second-story jobs or stick-ups or anything like that."

"I understand," smiled Lovo. Already his quick mind had seen the picture of Tony's former activities. "And I think you may be very valuable to me in time. But you'll have to start at the bottom, of course, and I'll have to test you awhile first. I'll give you a job driving a truck at a hundred dollars a week."

Tony's heart sank. Driving a truck—he who had never been a roustabout but always a white collar gangster, who had never done any but the smoother and more gentlemanly types of gangster activity, and who had been somewhat of a figure in that small-time prewar gangland. But then these were different times and this was a much bigger game that he wanted to sit in.

"All right, sir," he assented. "But I don't want to do that any longer than I have to; there's plenty of common hoods that can be hired for jobs like that."

"You can shoot?" queried Lovo softly.

"Yes; I have."

"In the army, you mean?"

"Yes. And before I went into it."

"Interesting. No, I don't think you'll be driving a truck very long.... Got a gat now?"

"No, sir."

"We'll furnish you one.... You broke?"

"No, sir. I got about six grand of my own."

"Good. But don't let anybody else know it. Rent a safety deposit box tomorrow at that bank across the street and put it away. Never carry a lot of money around with you; it isn't healthy. Be here at noon tomorrow."

And Tony became a real modern gangster, a member of a big, powerful, wealthy organization that collected more than a third of all the profits that came from liquor, gambling and vice in America's second largest city and a considerable territory around it.

Tony spent most of his time driving alcohol from the innumerable stills that were being operated for Lovo in all the western suburbs to the big plant in Cicero where the whisky was manufactured. He was never molested by officers; they were all being paid by Lovo. His only concern was hijackers, who were beginning to become active. But he always carried two guns—a six-shooter and an automatic—in the truck and his lips tightened when he thought of hijackers.

At last an idea came to Tony. Why not have all the trucks equipped with enclosed cabs of steel and bulletproof glass so that an attacked driver could defend himself and his employer's goods with impunity? He went to Lovo and presented his idea.

"Great!" approved the gang leader. "I'll have it carried out at once. Here's a little bonus." From a thick roll he peeled off a hundred-dollar bill and tossed it across the desk. "I think you've driven a truck long enough, Tony. Be here at nine tonight; I've got a little job I want you to handle for me."

Tony returned to Lovo's office promptly at the appointed hour, feeling considerably elated. He had been promoted; he was going to get somewhere in this racket yet.

"The North Side gang's been cutting into my territory," explained Lovo, and his dark eyes glittered with a hard, vindictive light that Tony had never seen in them before. "I don't want to open up a big battle with them if I can help it. But I do want to throw a good scare into the saloonkeepers and hold them in line so they won't buy from anybody else. Now, here's what you're to do."

Tony listened carefully to his instructions, then hurried out with both his hip pockets very heavy. Fifteen minutes later he walked slowly into a large corner saloon in a rather ratty district. Lounging against the bar, he ordered a drink and paid for it. Then he walked nonchalantly down the room until he finally stood at the end of the bar, a position from which his eyes and guns would command the situation without possibility of upset.

In addition to himself and the owner, who was acting as his own bartender, there were perhaps forty men in the place, the loud, rough, mixed crowd that one would expect to find in a frowsy saloon in a cheap neighborhood. Deliberately Tony lit a cigarette, then with an incredibly quick movement he pulled his two guns. One he pointed down the bar, while the muzzle of the other roved about.

"Step right up, boys, and have a drink," he commanded quietly. "It's all on me."

They stared at him in amazement. But the guns looked ominous and, though obviously puzzled by the whole proceeding, the men flocked to the bar. The surprised owner nervously began serving, his glance often wandering to that revolver pointing fixedly at him.

After that first drink, Tony quietly commanded them to have another, and another and another. Whisky, gin, wine, beer—it was all swilled down until not another drink was left in the house. Then, with one of the guns, Tony motioned the owner to him.

"Don't buy any more stuff from that North Side outfit," he commanded in a low tone. "Stick with Lovo, where you started. If you don't, the next time I drop in one of these pets of mine is liable to go off. Good night!"

He backed out of the door, ran half a block, and dodged through an alley to the next street, where he hailed a taxi.

chapter 8

"You did a good job, Tony," commended Lovo when the boy reported the next morning. "I think it was awfully funny, your telling that saloonkeeper that it was all on you."

He threw back his head and laughed heartily. Tony's eyes narrowed.

"I didn't tell you I said that."

"No," admitted the gang leader. "But I know you did say it. You see, I had two other men there last night— to help you in case you needed it."

That explanation did not fool Tony for a moment. Those other men had been there to watch him, to see how he worked on a high-pressure job. Johnny Lovo was even more clever than Tony had given him credit for.

"You carried it off in great shape, kid. I'll have some more particular little jobs for you soon. And from now on your salary's two hundred a week."

Tony's new assignment was to visit saloons, keeping in line those who were already customers of Lovo, and trying to persuade the others to change their business to—the Lovo organization. It was a dangerous assignment but Tony loved it. Undeniably he had a gift of gab far beyond the average boy of his education and environment. And he could put the screws on with a smiling suavity that was little short of masterful. His success was surprising.

As he made his rounds one afternoon, a heavy car screeched to a halt at the curb beside him.

"Hey, you!" snarled an ugly voice. "C'mere."

Tony turned. There were four toughs in the car and the ugly snouts of sawed-off shotguns pointed directly at him. For an instant he felt the helpless, strangling sensation of a drowning man, past events rushing through his mind in the same kaleidoscopic fashion. Was this to be his end, an ignominious death at the ruthless hands of a band of thugs? To attempt to draw his own gun would mean certain death; so would an attempt to escape. There was nothing to do but obey. He crossed the sidewalk to the side of the car.

"Well?" he said coldly and there was about him not the slightest suggestion of fear.

"Listen, you!" snarled the apparent leader, an ugly brute with a flattened, misshapen nose and tiny, granite-like gray eyes. "You're goin' around tryin' to steal the North Side outfit's business, tryin' to make the saloonkeepers switch over and buy from Lovo. Well, cut it out, see? We're only goin' to warn you this once, like we have the other Lovo men. Then you'll be taken for a ride."

The car raced away, leaving Tony staring after it. Taken for a ride—so that was what they threatened him with, the most feared of all gangland reprisals. A ride always ended in death—the body was usually found out in the country somewhere—but what happened before death was oftentimes an awful thing. Bodies of gangsters had been found without ears, without tongues, hacked in various ghoulish ways, bearing all too plainly evidences of dreadful torture before bullets had mercifully ended it all. But then that was the purpose of a ride—it was as much a warning to others as it was a wreaking of vengeance upon one man.

It was characteristic of Tony that he did not halt his activities after this warning. But he added another gun to his equipment and kept them handy at all times; he watched his step with greater care than he ever had before and he resumed his old practice of having an armed bodyguard follow him.

At noon one day, Tony received a rush call from Lovo to come to the leader's office immediately. He found Johnny seated at his desk, his swarthy face pale and set, in his black eyes the bright ominous glitter that can be seen in the eyes of a rattlesnake when it is about to strike.

"Sit down," commanded Lovo. There was no greeting; no smile. Tony knew immediately that something serious either had happened or was about to happen. "Al Swali's been taken for a ride."

Tony gasped and his own swarthy countenance paled slightly. Al Swali was one of Lovo's best men, a man who had been on the same sort of assignment as himself. So those thugs had made good their threat!

"They found his body out the other side of Melrose Park," continued Lovo bitterly. "Tied hand and foot with wire and shot a dozen times. He was identified from some papers in his pockets and they telephoned me a few minutes ago."

"It was the North Side gang, that got him, of course," said Tony in a low tone, and told Lovo of the warning that had been given him a few days before.

"I suppose you're marked to ride next," said Lovo with matter-of-fact resentment. "Well, they're not goin' to get you, nor anybody else in my mob. I'm goin' to put the fear of God in 'em and do it quick. Are you game to help me pull something daring?"

"Absolutely."

"Good. If you put it over, there'll be a grand in it for you. Be here at eight in a tux... I Have you got one?"

"No."

"Well, buy one—with all the trimmings. You'll probably need it often. You got to be fixed up fashionable to pull the job I'm planning.... Don't forget—eight o'clock here and be all togged out. I'll have a gun girl here to go with you."

Tony hurried out, feeling strangely excited. He knew that it was a killing on for that night and there is always a thrill—even to an experienced gunman—in going after such important game. And Lovo had said that a gun girl would go with him. He wondered if it would be *the* gun girl, that noted one about which he had heard so much, that striking brunette that he had seen in the cabaret the night he knocked down Captain Flanagan for insulting Vyvyan. It wasn't likely, of course, yet it was a possibility. He looked forward to the night's activities with keen anticipation.

He approached Lovo's office that evening with his heart pounding. Would it be *the* gun girl? He certainly hoped so; he'd always wanted to know her. In conformity with orders, he was attired in a dinner jacket "with all the trimmings." And quite handsome he looked, with his erect, well-built figure and thoroughly barbered countenance.

He knocked, then turned the knob and crossed the threshold. Lovo was seated at his desk just as Tony had left him hours before.. And by his side sat *the* gun girl. Tony recognized her instantly and a gasp of admiration caught in his throat. God! she was beautiful! A—lithe, slender brunette with a superb figure cunningly revealed by the close-fitting, very low cut evening gown. Its sheer whiteness provided a startling contrast with ' her vivid dark beauty, the ivory tint of her skin, the long, fashionably coiffed hair so black that its depths held bluish glints like fine gunmetal, the great dark eyes with their hints of hidden inner fires, the beautifully shaped red mouth.

"Jane, Tony," introduced Lovo briefly. "Sit down, kid. You look great."

Tony sank into a chair, feeling trembly under the appraising stare of the girl's great dark eyes.

"This is a big job I'm trusting you to handle tonight, Tony," said Lovo. "Perhaps it's too big for you. But I don't think so and you've proven yourself so damn loyal to me that I'm going to give you a crack at it. Of course, if you fail, you're through with me and I'll have somebody else do it. But I'm not expecting you to fail. *I want you to get Jerry Hoffman.*"

"Jerry Hoffman!" exclaimed Tony. The girl said nothing, not even indicating the surprise she must have felt.

"Exactly," continued Lovo. "Jerry Hoffman, the biggest guy on the North Side and leader of that whole mob. Right now, there's nobody big enough to step into his shoes and his death will ruin the whole outfit. They'll know, of course, that some of my mob did it but they won't know exactly who pulled the job—that is, if you two are as clever as I think you are—and his being bumped off will throw 'em into such a panic that I think they'll be afraid to try any jobs on us for a long time. It's high stakes we're playing for, folks, but the reward will make the risk worthwhile."

"All right," said Tony shortly. "I'm game. What's the plan?"

"I've found out that Hoffman is giving a little party tonight at the Embassy Club."

"*Him* —at the Embassy Club?" exclaimed the girl incredulously, speaking for the first time. And her voice— rich, full, throaty, gave Tony as big a thrill as did her appearance.

"Oh, yes," answered Lovo with a short laugh. "Surprising the places you can buy your way into—if you've got the price. Well, he's giving a little party there tonight. Very select affair, couple of judges and an assistant district attorney or two and so on. He won't have the slightest suspicion of being attacked there and in that company, so he won't have his bodyguards around, and as he doesn't know either one of you by sight it ought to be easy for you to get him. I'm not going to give you any orders as to how to handle the job. Work it out on the spot as you think best. *But get him!* Got a gat on you, Tony?"

"Certainly."

"Give it to me. Jane does the gat carrying tonight—she's got it on her now. When you're ready and want it, she'll give it to you. The minute you've pulled the job, slip it back to her *at once* and she'll hide it again. Then if some wise guy should recognize you and have you frisked, you haven't got a thing on you. See?"

Reluctantly Tony passed over his own gun, accepted the admission card to the Embassy Club which Lovo handed him, and escorted the gun girl out to the waiting limousine which Lovo had provided.

The Embassy Club was the most exclusive of the expensive night clubs which had sprung up since the war—and Prohibition. As well as providing food, dancing and entertainment, it sold the best of liquors and one had to have a card to gain admittance. Where Lovo had secured the card which now rested in his well-filled pin seal wallet, Tony had no idea, but as the gang leader had said—money would do amazing things.

A large table, handsomely set for ten or twelve, indicated where the Hoffman party was to be and Tony maneuvered the head waiter into seating him and his companion directly across from it and not more than thirty feet away. It was a splendid position, too, for a strategic retreat, being in a direct line with the door and not far from it.

Tony felt a little nervous as he ordered. This was the first time he had ever worked with a gun girl and he found it a strange sensation not to have his own gun where he could reach for it whenever he wished. But Jane was as calm as though they were there bent only on pleasure and her calmness finally soothed him. God! she was beautiful! What he would give to have a woman like that for his very own.

They chatted about this and that as they ate. But she did most of the talking. Tony was quite content to just sit and watch her, drinking in her beauty. The little pauses that fell between them now and then were tense to the point of being electrical. Tony, believed he was making progress.

There was considerable hubbub when the Hoffman party came in. It required the attentions of the owner, the head waiter and half the other waiters to see that the party was properly seated. Truly, money—regardless of its source—commanded respect and service.

Tony stiffened and his keen glance surveyed the situation. He recognized Hoffman immediately—a tall, rather heavy man with a red face and sandy hair. Tony scanned the rest of the party carefully but he could find none that looked like a gunman or a bodyguard. Now Hoffman probably felt entirely safe there in that exclusive cabaret in the company of men whose importance was unquestioned. It would be a cinch to bump him off there; the only thing was to pull the job at the proper time. Tony waited, smoking one cigarette after another with an outward calmness that was the result of iron self-control. Jane was chatting gaily about nothing in particular and occasionally laughed lightly for no reason. Tony realized that she was playing her part well, giving their table an air of casualness and gaiety. He tried to join in with her but; he was naturally a silent type and now he could hardly keep his eyes off the man who was soon to be his target.

Champagne corks were popping at that other table and there was much loud laughing. Tony called for his check and paid it. Then the main lights were snapped off, a spotlight centering on the small dance floor. A brash, overdressed young man stepped out into its glow and began telling about the show that was to follow, interspersing his remarks with supposedly funny wisecracks. Now was the time to pull the job, when everybody's attention was centered on the show.

Tony looked at Jane and nodded slightly. She gave him a look of understanding, then, with every appearance of affection, caught his right hand and gently maneuvered it beneath the table. His hand found her knee, rested there. And he thrilled at the contact. But she did not shrink. Then he felt cold steel against his flesh and his eager fingers clutched an automatic. His thumb slipped off the safety catch and he waited.

Some woman sang a comic song that made Tony laugh—even in the tensity of the moment—then the chorus came on. While doing a fancy dance routine, they sang at the top of their voices, the jazz band blared madly, and the customers beat time with little wooden mallets provided for the purpose. The din was tremendous.

Tony brought the gun up into his lap, then cautiously reached out, holding the weapon close beside the table and well below the level of its top. Nobody yet had been seated on that side of them; at the moment not even a waiter was there. Tony took careful aim and fired three times, so rapidly that the reports almost merged into each other. He saw Hoffman slump forward as he jerked the pistol under the table and slipped it back to Jane. Her fingers were cool and steady as she took it from him.

The noise of the shots had penetrated even that din, of course, and there was a sudden commotion. The main lights were snapped back on and everybody stood up, staring horror-stricken at that table where Hoffman lay slumped low in his chair, an ever widening spot of crimson disfiguring his snowy shirtfront. Then began a mad scramble to get away before the police should arrive. These people had no wish to be questioned about a murder, and have their names and perhaps their pictures in the papers.

Tony and Jane were in the van of that frantic, fear-struck mob. Within less than two minutes they were comfortably seated in-'

their limousine and were being driven rapidly away from the scene. Tony took a long breath.

"Well, that's done," he said calmly. Now that it was all over, he felt calm, even gay. "We've done a good night's work for ourselves. And for Lovo. He won't forget it either, I think. But say, girlie, you sure have got guts."

"A person has to have to get along these days," answered Jane Conley quietly.

He reached out and caught her hand, fondled her fingers. It thrilled him to see that she made no effort to pull away.

"You and I will probably work together quite a bit from now," he said huskily. "Why can't we be good pals and—play together, too?"

"Perhaps we can."

Obeying a sudden irresistible impulse, he caught her in his arms and kissed her, with all the frantic ardor of a strong, eager passion long repressed. And she made no effort to resist.

chapter 9

Jerry Hoffman's death created a sensation and for days the city was rife with conjectures as to who could have carried out such a daring murder plot. But the police and gangland both had a good idea as to who was responsible. The dicks took Johnny Lovo down to headquarters and questioned him for half a day but he told them nothing beyond proving an alibi for himself. Nor did he give the impression of defiantly holding back something. On the contrary, he blandly and smilingly convinced them that he actually knew nothing. But the North Side gang was far from convinced and some day they meant to have vengeance for the death of their chief.

Neither Tony nor Jane was ever mentioned in connection with the affair. Lovo gave them a thousand dollars each and thanked them profusely, promising to let them handle any other little jobs he might have in the future. In the meantime he sent an enormous and elaborate floral piece bearing his card to Jerry Hoffman's garish and expensive funeral and gave Tony various assignments in connection with the gang's activities. But he didn't send Tony back to the interesting but perilous task of proselytizing saloonkeepers—he considered the boy too valuable an aid now to risk in such reckless fashion. No, Tony had become a staff officer now. His work consisted mainly in relaying Lovo's orders to the powerful leader's henchmen and in receiving reports that Lovo himself was too busy to hear. There was no detail of the gang's operation that Tony did not come to know.

He spent all his spare time in pursuing Jane Conley. And the more he saw of her, the more fascinated he became with her. Yet there was something elusive about her. He could never feel that he had a definite grasp upon her. Yet he finally got his courage up to the point of proposing that they take a flat together.

"I'm not interested in marriage," she answered with a shake of her shapely head.

"Neither am I," agreed Tony quickly. "But who said anything about marriage? I said I thought it would be nice for us to have a flat together."

Again she shook her head.

"I've never lived with a man."

"Well, you might find it a pleasant experience."

"Yes," she admitted frankly, looking him straight in the eye. "And then again, I might not. I'm afraid it would be too—intimate; that people, even if they were very much in love—when they started, would surely tire each other finally."

"Is there—somebody else?"

"Not particularly."

"But there is somebody?" he persisted jealously.

She laughed lightly. "There is always somebody else. Any girl knows more than one man and often likes more than one very much."

"Then you do like me a little?" He was at her side, with her hand caught in both of his.

She nodded.

"And you will think about what I proposed?"

"Yes, I'll think about it."

And with that he had to be content. This Jane Conley was a very strange woman, he reflected. He often wondered who she was, where she came from. As much as he had been with her, he really didn't know her at all. And he knew enough about women to realize that that very mystery and elusiveness was one of the main reasons why she fascinated him so intensely.

But he had enough on his mind without troublesome love affairs. Contrary to expectations, the North Side gang had found a new leader and apparently an able one, a wily little Italian rightly named Schemer Bruno.

Rumor had it that he was reorganizing things in every direction and preparing to set out on a campaign of reprisals and business-getting that would set the city by the ears. That he was utterly ruthless and intended carrying on with gusto the feuds begun by his predecessor was proven by the fact that another of Johnny Lovo's best men was taken for a ride, his body discovered out in the country with a scrawled note, *In Memory of Hoffman,* tacked to his chest with the blade of a pocketknife.

"I tell you, Tony, I don't like this," said Lovo after the man's body bearing its gruesome message was brought in.

"Not gettin' scared, are you?" demanded Tony. He talked to Lovo now with the freedom of a privileged counselor.

"Hell, no!" snapped the gang leader, but he talked like a man who is assuming a falsely ferocious air to maintain his own courage. "But just the same I don't like it. It may be you next—or me. I don't want to spend the rest of my life having somebody shot and trying to keep somebody else from shooting me or my employees."

"Forget it!" advised Tony. "It's all in the game. We'll fight 'em to a finish and get this Schemer guy too if necessary."

"No, not yet. Maybe he'll quit now. I don't want to spend all my time in a war; it takes too much time away from making money."

Tony departed from that interview much disgusted with Johnny Lovo. He did not realize the essential differences between them; that Lovo was merely a shrewd and unscrupulous man willing to do anything for money; that he was much more a business man than a fighter; and that he had had none of Tony's war experience which had taught the younger man such a supreme contempt for human life.

Then for the first time Tony actually saw the close contact which exists between crime and the law. Lovo was summoned to the District Attorney's office and he took Tony along as a sort of body-guard and aide-de-camp. The District Attorney was a little man with a flat nose, an undershot belligerent jaw and mean little eyes.

"This shooting has got to be stopped," he barked at Lovo. "It's—"

"But I'm paying—"

"Of course you are. And you'll keep on paying if you want to keep on doing business. It isn't your business that I'm objecting *to;* it's this damned shooting that's going on among you. It's getting the city a bad name and what's more important, the newspapers are

beginning to ride me and my administration. I don't want to inter-
fere with you boys any more than is absolutely necessary, but this
killing has got to be stopped."

"I'm willing. It's that North Side outfit."

"And they say it's you. I had this Schemer Bruno in here for an
hour this morning and he promised his mob would do no more
killing if yours didn't. So that's settled, then. Now I don't want to
hear of any more gang wars."

For six months there was peace, that is, on the surface. There were
no killings but fist-fighting and stabbings occurred with too great
frequency to be accidental. The rivalry for business was becoming
keener and more bitter daily, and all sides knew that it was merely
a question of time until somebody blew the lid off and started the
old feuds all over again. The two South Side factions also were
beginning to meddle in districts which belonged to other gangs and
on the near west side a crowd of five brothers had suddenly set up
in the bootlegging and allied rackets with a strong gang of their
own.

Tony was growing restive from inaction. And he was deeply
resentful of many things, of the fact that the last murder of a Lovo
man was still unavenged, of the fact that other gangs were beginning to encroach upon the Lovo territory and that they were not
being challenged by the bullets that should be poured into them. He
had just about decided to begin a lone war of reprisal when the lid
was blown off.

He and Johnny Lovo were dining at a table in the ground floor
restaurant of the hotel where Lovo had his headquarters and which
he owned. Suddenly there was a rapid staccato rattle of shots from
outside somewhere, the tinkling crash of shattered plate glass windows and the spiteful whizzing of bullets. With one sweep of his
arm, Tony overturned the table and dragged Lovo down behind it.
He had recognized that peculiar stuttering of those guns outside.
Machine guns! Why hadn't somebody used them before? Why had-
n't he, an expert machine gunner, thought of them and brought
them into play in this other war that was for money only? Well, if
that was the way they were going to play now, he'd give them a
nasty dose of their own medicine.

That shooting had been a direct attempt to get Johnny Lovo himself. It was the most daring move of the enemy so far. And it had
been partly successful. Lovo had been hit in the shoulder. It wasn't

a serious wound but the fact remained that he had been hit for the first time and it brought a hunted look into his eyes that remained there forever after. Johnny wasn't a warrior when his own person was involved; his nerves weren't constructed to stand the strain.

That attempt to kill Lovo made Tony furious. He felt that it was a gesture of contempt which must not be allowed to remain unanswered if the Lovo organization was to continue and to endure. Without saying a word to anybody, he managed to purchase a machine gun himself. Then one night he set out on a little war of his own.

The headquarters of the North Side gang was upstairs over a florist's shop which had been the property and hobby of the gang's first and greatest leader, the famous Tommy Martin, who had been shot down among, his own flowers—the first postwar gang leader to die from the bullets of an enemy. The shop, which was directly across the street from a large cathedral, was located on a thoroughfare which was dark and quiet at night.

Sitting in the tonneau of the car with his machine gun on his lap, Tony ordered his chauffeur to drive slowly past the shop. As the car moved deliberately along, Tony lifted the machine gun to his shoulder—it was one of the new type that are operated much as a rifle—and riddled the front of the shop, both upstairs and down. There had been a light on the second floor which went off the moment he started firing and he had no means of knowing if he hit anybody. But he had certainly done plenty of damage, he reflected happily as the car raced away from the scene. He'd given them as good as they sent, and with their own weapon. Since machine guns had been introduced into the war, the score was even.

chapter 10

At first Tony had considered that long scar on the left side of his face a blessing because of the change it had made in his appearance. But now, he was beginning to regard it as a curse. It was making him a marked man. Already he was known through the underworld, not only to the members of the Lovo gang but to those of other mobs, as "Scarface Tony." And to be so well known that he could be easily identified was distinctly not a part of his plans.

He felt, too, that that scar might be hurting his suit with Jane Conley, the gun girl. Women could not make themselves love men who had disfiguring marks of any kind and that scar, even though it was becoming less noticeable as time went on, was not a thing of beauty.

He and Jane were the best of friends, often going places together and seeing a great deal of each other. Yet he felt that he was actually no closer to her than he had been the first time they met the night they had disposed of Jerry Hoffman. But the lure of her was growing upon him more and more, if such a thing were possible.

"Listen, girlie," he said one night, "I love you—more than I could ever tell you; I'm not much good at talkin'. But all I want is a chance to prove it. Please say 'yes' to that proposition I made you a long time ago."

Jane looked him straight in the eye for a moment and the directness of her gaze was rather disconcerting.

"All right," she answered. "We'll look around tomorrow for a place."

"You'll do it?" he cried, almost beside himself with elation.

"For one month—on trial. If at the end of that time I am not pleased with—everything, I am to leave and you are to say nothing, not even seeing me again if I ask you not to. Those are my conditions. Do you accept them?"

"Yes."

"Very well; it's a bargain."

"And if you are pleased with—everything?" he queried.

"The arrangement will probably last some time," she answered quietly.

Tony went away from the house that night, almost choking with triumph. At last he had won; that glorious creature was about to become his—even, if only for a month. But he meant to make things so pleasant that the arrangement would last much longer.

But he said nothing about it to Lovo when they met next morning. In the first place, it was a private matter and nobody else's business; and in the second, the gang leader was obviously preoccupied. Tony watched him pace nervously around the office, his unseeing gaze now on the ceiling, now on the floor, with a funny little sense of fright catching at his heart. What was troubling Lovo?

"I want to talk to you, Tony," said the other finally. "Sit down."

Tony took his place on the other side of the desk, feeling an odd sense of drama as though important events were about to transpire. Finally Lovo sat down himself in his big chair and lit another cigar.

"I've heard about your shooting up the florist shop the other night," he began.

"Yes?" said Tony uneasily. He wondered if he was to be sharply reprimanded.

"It was daring and all that but terribly dangerous. You must learn not to risk yourself like that."

"I—I'll try. But there's a lot of fun in pulling a job like that."

"I suppose so," assented Lovo. "For those that like it. Well, I'm not one of them. I'd rather be peaceable and make money. When they drag in machine guns, it's a bit too much. I've got plenty of money, Tony; more than I can ever spend if I use common sense. I think I'll take a trip, to Monte Carlo or Havana or some other gay sporting place where life is pleasant."

"For how long?"

"Years. In fact, I doubt very much if I shall ever return."

"But the mob! You can't let it break up and go to pieces—"

"It would be a shame to let such a complete organization wreck itself, wouldn't it? . Well, can't somebody else run it?"

"Certainly." Then remembering to whom he was talking, he added: "Perhaps not as well as you've run it, but they could hold the crowd together and keep things moving. And there's so much jack laying around just waiting to be picked up."

His voice almost became a groan as he remembered and mentioned the large illicit profits waiting to be garnered.

"I know," assented Lovo. "I'm not through with those profits yet myself.... Listen, Tony, do you think you could run this mob?"

"I know I could," answered the young man eagerly. "I wish you'd give me the chance."

"I'm going to, It's a heavy responsibility for a young fellow or even for an old one. But I'm going to take a chance on you and I believe you'll make good. You're to send half the net profits to me every month wherever I direct. If my payments don't come through regularly, of course I'll have to come back and—make other arrangements!" Their eyes met as he said that and it was evident that they understood each other completely. "Of the other half, you're to keep two-thirds of it and give the other third to your first lieutenant, Steve Libati."

"You want him to work that close to me?" asked Tony. He disliked Libati intensely.

"Yes. He's much older at the game than you are and Can give you good advice. Besides, he's always been completely loyal to me and I know he would never do anything that would hurt the organization. If—anything should happen to you, he is to take command."

"Does he know about all this?"

"No. But I'm going to tell him in an hour or two, after you and I have gone over some details."

For two hours the gang leader and his successor, discussed various aspects of the mob and its activities. Tony merely assented to whatever Lovo said but his own mind was formulating rapidly a plan of campaign, an aggressive, ruthless campaign that would leave the Lovo organization in command of the field. His eyes glinted as he thought of the many daring moves he wanted to make.

At last Steve Libati was called in and apprised of the situation. He was an ugly brute in the late thirties, a gangster of the old school, the type that wore sweaters and shapeless checked caps and lounged in front of frowsy corner saloons with a cigarette dangling from one corner of their ugly mouths while they talked hoarsely from the other. He had hard gray eyes and a nose bent slightly to one side and a mean mouth that sneered easily and nastily.

Tony disliked him intently and he had never evidenced any particular affection for Tony. They represented two entirely different epochs in gangland, and had practically nothing in common. Steve was of the prewar "strong-arm" type, who knew nothing except the law of might. Tony was of the dapper, businesslike, postwar type that went in for efficiency and regular business administration in crime, and that handled its necessary rough stuff with a breath-taking speed and thoroughness that accomplished the end without leaving, any traces of the perpetrators.

Furthermore, Tony had none of Lovo's faith in either Steve's ability or his loyalty. He had never seen the fellow do anything that proved either one. And he resented having the man handed to him on a plate and being told to make the best of it. But already he had resolved one thing—if he and Steve didn't get along well together, he intended to rid himself of the fellow. There were ways....

"Well, kid, we'll hit it off together in great shape, won't we?" exclaimed Steve with a great show of heartiness when the conditions of Lovo's virtual abdication had been explained to him. But there was a sly look in his hard eyes and a patronizing note in his rough voice that angered Tony.

"I hope so," he said coldly and turned to say something to Lovo.

Tony walked out of the hotel in the grip of a strange mixture of emotions. He was elated, of course, at being elevated to command of the big Lovo organization— it furnished him with the break he had always wished for and which would give him a chance to make good in a big way and clean up. But he resented Steve Libati. The more he thought about him, the more he disliked and distrusted the fellow. He could see him only as a spy for Lovo and as a general meddler. Oh, well, that problem would work itself out in time.

He met Jane and they went flat-hunting together. He told her of his big promotion and she was as excited as a child over a new toy.

"What a marvelous opportunity!" she exclaimed over and over. "You ought to be able to clean up and retire in a couple of years."

"Who wants to retire?" he demanded. "I want to *live*. Just because I'm the boss don't mean that I'm goin' to hide myself in an office some place and let somebody else have all the fun. I'm goin' to be out on the firing, line myself every now and then. You and I are goin' to pull some more little jobs, girlie; don't forget it. And there's goin' to be plenty of jobs to be done. If I'm to run this mob, I'm goin' to *run* it, and no halfway business. Moreover, I'm either goin' to run the competition out of town or kill 'em off."

They found a handsome furnished apartment in a large building in a fashionable section. The rent was enormous but they both liked the place and Tony was a big shot now. They rented the place for one month and he paid the rent in cash. And the following day found them installed, Jane as tremulously happy as a bride on her honeymoon.

Lovo departed on Friday. Tony drove him to a small station on the far South Side where he took a train for New York. Thus, there were no reporters or photographers around and the public at large had, no inkling that he was gone. Tony wanted to have everything running smoothly and have his own position and leadership thoroughly established before Lovo's absence was known.

Returning to Lovo's former office in the hotel to take command, Tony found Steve Libati comfortably established there, tilted back in Lovo's big chair, his feet on the desk, smoking a cigar.

"'Lo, kid!" he greeted Tony. And again his voice held that patronizing tone that made the younger man furious.

"Would you mind moving to another chair?" asked Tony coldly. "I want to sit there."

"Oh, all right." Steve shifted to another chair and Tony sat down at the desk. "As we're goin' to run the mob, I thought you and I ought to have a little talk."

"I don't know what about," retorted Tony coolly, picking up some papers and riffling through them in a This-is-my-busy-day manner. "I haven't decided on any definite plans yet. When I do, I'll let you know and give you your orders for your part in them."

For a long moment the two men stared at each other. Tony's right hand had moved quietly to his side coat pocket. He was waiting for definite insubordination. It did not come. Steve's mean eyes narrowed and his ugly mouth twisted into a snarl. Then he relaxed and forced a smile.

"All right," he said, "if that's the way you feel about it."

He picked up his hat and walked out. Tony had won the first tilt. But he realized that the inevitable serious trouble between them had only been postponed.

Tony worked hard the rest of that day and evening and all the next day and evening, getting things organized both in his head and on paper. The gang had been gradually falling lately, both in efficiency and income, because of Lovo's reluctance to carry out reprisals. There was much to do. The first thing was to carry out successfully two or three daring coups—preferably killings—against the enemy so as to give the boys some confidence and pride in their own outfit. Then would come the serious organization work that meant big profits. Within sixty days, Tony meant to have those profits bigger than they had ever been under Lovo's leadership.

It was almost ten o'clock on Saturday night when Al, the little rat-faced gangster who acted as guard and doorman for the office, came in to Tony.

"Captain Flanagan's here," he announced.

Tony looked up quickly.

"Who?" he demanded.

"Captain Flanagan, chief of the dicks at headquarters,"

A grim smile played about Tony's lips'. So Flanagan was here! Well he remembered that bullying officer whom he had knocked down in the cabaret for insulting Vyvyan and who thereafter had practically run him out of town. The shoe was on the other foot now. Tony took an ugly automatic out of a drawer and laid it on the desk within easy reach.

"Show him in!" he ordered grimly.

chapter 11

Captain Flanagan, chief of detectives, came striding into the new gang leader's office with the confident, arrogant air of one who is on familiar ground and who, though not expecting a warm welcome, realizes that his position demands a certain courtesy and respect.

Scarface Tony, seated behind the desk to which he had just succeeded, with his right hand resting lightly on the automatic lying on its top, watched the official enter. And a blast of rage as fierce as the heat from a suddenly opened furnace door swept through him. But the main thing he wondered was whether or not Flanagan would recognize him.

Flanagan evidently did not see in this smartly dressed man with a livid scar traversing the left side of his hard face from ear to jaw the handsome boy who had knocked him down less than three years before and whom he later had practically run out of the city. For there was no hint of recognition in the officer's granite gray eyes as he pushed his derby to the back of his head and with his big feet planted widely apart and his hands thrust deep into his pockets, stood staring at the new leader of the powerful Lovo gang.

"Where's Johnny?" demanded Flanagan.

"Mr. Lovo is not in." Tony's eyes were as coldly impersonal as his tone.

"I can see that," snapped Flanagan, his cruel mouth twisting angrily. "I ain't blind. Where is he?"

"Out of town. And he won't be back for some time."

Flanagan snorted.

"Quit kiddin'," he snarled. "Johnny's always in on the first of the month—for me."

"Oh! I see. Just a moment."

From one of the desk drawers Tony produced a small notebook which contained the gang's pay-off list, the names of those officials, high and slow, who had to be padded, and the amount of the monthly bit of each. The list was carefully arranged in alphabetical order and Tony soon ascertained that the Lovo mob's monthly contribution to the happiness and prosperity of Captain Flanagan was $500.

Tony dropped the little book back in the desk drawer. Then he pulled out a fat roll of money and peeling off five $100 bills, threw them across the desk in a manner most contemptuous.

"There you are. But remember that we want some service for all this jack we pay out."

"As if you didn't get it," snarled Flanagan, snatching up the money and stuffing it into his pocket. "What I could do to this outfit if I wanted would be a sight."

"Yes, I suppose so," admitted Tony reflectively. "Yet we boys have our own methods for discouraging our enemies."

"What do you mean?"

"Nothing," answered Tony calmly, but he could see that his veiled warning had registered. "And now, Flanagan, I think it might be a good idea for you and I to have a little talk. I'm Tony Camonte. And from now on I'm in command of this mob."

"You!"

"Me," asserted Tony solemnly. "Johnny Lovo left yesterday for a long vacation. He may be back sometime but I don't think so. He's got plenty of dough and he's tired of this racket. Of course he's still interested but he turned the active control of things over to me."

"Won't some of his other lieutenants question your authority?"

"Maybe. But they won't question it more than once." Tony patted the automatic and the glance he gave Flanagan was significant.

"Well!" exclaimed the captain. "This *is* news. Though I been wonderin' lately if Johnny hadn't lost his nerve or somep'm. This mob's been pretty quiet for a while."

"Too damn quiet!" agreed Tony, his eyes snapping with energetic resolve. "But all that's goin' to be changed now and changed damn quick."

"That'll be interesting to the other mob leaders."

"Let 'em find it out. They don't have to be told anything. I don't want this change spread around or leakin' into the papers. But I wanted you to know about it so that if I give you a ring some day and want a favor done in a hurry you'll know who I am."

Tony sneered at the captain's broad back as Flanagan departed. There, he thought, was a good example of the men who are supposed to stand between the lawless and the law-abiding citizenry. Trafficking for his own profit with those he had sworn to hunt down. That was the nub of the whole matter, *Money.* The underworld now was too wealthy to allow itself to be hunted down. But even a cop was human, thought Tony; how could people be so fool-ish as to expect him to do his duty for five thousand a year—and sometimes less— when not doing it would make him twenty-five thousand and oftentimes more.

A knock at the door roused him from his reflections on cops in general and Flanagan in particular.

"Come in," he called brusquely and had the automatic trained on the portal before one could turn the knob.

But it was only Al, the little rat-faced outer doorkeeper.

"Somebody just phoned on that back room wire at the cigar store downstairs," he announced, "and said that Charlie Martino, one of our truck drivers, was hijacked and shot a little bit ago. He's at a garage in Maywood now—here's the address—and whoever phoned said he needs a doctor bad."

"Wonder why he didn't give 'em one of our numbers up here to call," Tony said.

"Prob'ly didn't want to give 'em to strangers. Charlie's a good, reliable boy, boss," said Al pleadingly, "I know him well."

"If it's true, I want to help him all I can," said Tony. "But most likely it's that North Side mob tryin' to put me on the spot. We got to go careful on this."

Within five minutes—so thoroughly systematized was the Lovo organization and its operations—Tony was in possession of Charlie Martino's scheduled movements for the evening and also of his past record with the gang. The latter was unblemished, both as to loyalty and ability, over a period of two years. This evening Charlie was supposed to be bringing a load of raw grain alcohol from Melrose Park, a suburb where almost every house had a big still and the Italian inhabitants were making comfortable little fortunes by "cooking alky" for the big syndicates, into a warehouse near the gang's headquarters in Cicero. A call to Melrose Park revealed that he had picked up his load and departed according to schedule. But another call revealed that he had not arrived at the warehouse. It looked as though the plea for assistance was genuine.

"Tell six or seven of the boys downstairs to bring around a coupla cars and plenty of gats," snapped Tony, his black eyes glittering with excitement, though his voice was as cool and calm as if he were giving a telephony number. "I'm going out and have a look at this."

Al hurried away, to relay orders to the cigar store downstairs which was a sort of squad room for the gang. Tony called a safe doctor—one of those rare physicians who, for enormous fees, will attend the underworld's gunshot wounds without going through the prescribed formality of reporting them to the police—and, giving him the address in Maywood, ordered him to proceed there immediately. Then he grabbed his automatic and hurried downstairs.

In the dark alley back of the hotel—which was the gang's headquarters because Lovo owned it—he found a group of shadowy figures moving about two large dark touring cars with drawn side curtains. The clank of metal came to his ears as he advanced. They were loading in the machine guns, of course.

"Ready, boys?" he inquired. "Good! Let's go!"

He leaped into the tonneau of one car. Men piled in around him and in front and he saw the other men climbing into the car ahead. Motors roared into pulsing life and with a whine of racing engines the two carloads of expert gunmen sped away on their errand of either mercy or murder. Tony hoped it would prove to be both.

To his left he could discern in the gloom the ugly snouts of two machine guns. He reached over and pulled one of them into his lap.

"I'm with these babies like some people with a car," he said with a laugh. "I feel safer when I'm at the wheel."

A block away from the garage which was their objective, they cut put the engines and coasted the rest of the way. But their practiced eyes found nothing suspicious on any side. Abruptly the engines roared again and the two big cars, bristling with the most modern death-dealing machinery, ready for anything, swept into the garage and ground to a halt.

A man in greasy mechanic's coveralls, came forward, wiping his hands on a bit of waste. Tony opened the door next to him and looked out.

"We had a call that there was a man here—hurt," he said brusquely.

"Yes. He's back there in my little office. A doctor just came to see him."

The man jerked a dirty thumb toward a small coupe which Tony recognized as belonging to the doctor he had summoned. The gang leader lifted his machine gun to the floor of the car and stepped out. But as he followed the other man across the grease-spotted concrete floor, his right hand was plunged deep into his side coat pocket and his keen glance was searching the shadows on all sides. Behind him, he knew that other keen glances were doing the same thing and that he was covered by an amazing amount of artillery.

As the two men entered the cluttered little space partitioned off from the rest of the building, the doctor looked up. He was a thin, nervous little man with a pallid complexion and shifty black eyes. But he knew his business, as many a live gangster could testify.

"Pretty serious," he said with a gesture toward his patient, who lay stretched out on a canvas cot, his eyes closed, his breathing slow and hoarse. "Shot twice . through the chest. He's lost a lot of blood. We ought to get him somewhere where I can Work on him."

"Can he be moved?" asked Tony.

"Yes. I'll give him a stimulant."

The doctor quickly filled a hypodermic needle from . some of the bottles in his grip and injected the contents into the patient's wrist. In a few moments the boy—he was little more than that—opened his eyes. Tony walked over to him.

"He's too weak to talk," cautioned the doctor.

Tony grasped his henchman's hand. Their glances met, held, and the boy's vacant stare changed to happy recognition.

"Was it the North Side outfit?" demanded Tony harshly. "Schemer Bruno's mob?"

The boy tried to speak but so much effort was beyond him. He nodded.

"All right, we'll see them, kid," promised Tony gruffly and gripped that limp hand hard.

The garage man's eyes widened when he heard that ominous threat of gangland vengeance. When Tony turned on him, he told his story quickly. Returning from towing a car out of a ditch, he had come upon the wounded boy lying at the side of a lonely road, and had brought him on to the garage. The boy had pleaded with him to call only a certain number, a request to which he had acceded.

"You see, I thought it was prob'ly a case that it was best not to make too much fuss about," he concluded.

"You've done well," Tony commended, and slipped him a $100 bill. ".How's your memory?"

"Terrible, boss," grinned the man with a knowing wink. "Why, I have to look up the number every time I want to phone my own house."

Tony grinned himself and slapped the man on the back. Money and power on one hand and lack of them on the other has a way of making people understand each other quickly and thoroughly.

They took the wounded boy back to a room in the hotel which was the gang's headquarters and the doctor went to work on him in an effort to save his life. Tony retired to his private office and sent for Steve Libati, the man whom Lovo had appointed as second in command of the gang during his absence and who, Tony realized, was very jealous of his position as chief. He felt that now was as good a time as any to give the man an important assignment, to test his ability and his loyalty.

chapter 12

Steve Libati came in looking somewhat sullen and defiant. A gangster of a somewhat older school than Tony, of the sweater-and-checked-cap era, he had never quite accustomed himself to the smooth, suave, businesslike methods of the modern, post-Prohibition gangsters. Though he now wore the best clothes and drove an expensive car, he still talked from one corner of his cruel mouth and, at times, revealed other distressing symptoms of having been a common street-corner thug.

"That North Side mob's at it again," said Tony, plunging immediately to the heart of the matter. "They hijacked one of our trucks of alky tonight and knocked off the driver. Kid named Charlie Martino. I took some of the boys and went out and got him a little bit ago. He's down the hall here now and Doc's workin' on him to try to keep him from croakin'. Happened between Maywood and Melrose Park. That's the first time that outfit has come that far into our territory and it's goin' to be the *last.*"

"Think you can stop 'em?" asked Libati calmly, his head cocked on one side and his left eye closed against the smoke curling upward from his cigarette.

"I'm *going* to stop 'em." Tony punctuated the statement with a sharp blow on the desk with his clenched fist. "If I have to have every man in the mob bumped off. Things have been too quiet lately; from now on, they're goin' to see action that'll curl their hair. Johnny thought that Jerry Hoffman bein' bumped off would ruin that mob but they found this Schemer Bruno guy and he's turned out to be the best leader since Tommy Martin, better than Jerry ever thought of bein'. From now on, the war's between that mob and this one; the others don't cut much ice.

"Now, Steve, bumpin' off small fry like Charlie is a nuisance but it don't really hurt a mob. You can always find plenty of kids who'll take a chance for the price. To ruin a mob, you gotta get the leaders, the brains of the outfit. And you can bet this Schemer guy knows that as well as we do. So it's just a matter of time till he takes a crack at me—or you. Well, I'm goin' to beat him to the draw and get him before he gets me. And I've picked you to do the job."

Steve tensed. His ugly features settled into an angry scowl.

"Why me?" he demanded.

"I gotta have somebody reliable that I can trust to handle it right."

"Why don't you do it yourself?"

For a long moment Tony stared at his subordinate while fury gathered in his eyes. He strangled it with an obvious effort.

"Because I don't choose to. As head of the mob, I think my duty is to stay in the background and run things."

Libati laughed sarcastically. Tony's eyes blazed.

"I could get Bruno," he snapped furiously, "and do it within forty-eight hours. Don't think I wouldn't like to. *And I will if necessary.* But with my position now, I feel I shouldn't take chances like that if I don't have to. Just the same, I'll never ask a man in this mob to do anything that I can't or won't do myself. I got Jerry Hoffman and I got others. A good many times I proved I got guts enough for anything. *But I never heard yet of you provin' that you had any.* Now's your chance."

Libati paled at the insinuation and his cruel mouth set in a nasty snarl. For a moment it looked as though he was going to pull a gun. Tony hoped he would, for he himself was ready and that would settle his problem of what to do with Steve Libati. But the fellow had sense enough to regain his self-control.

"You talk like you was the only big shot in this mob," he snarled. "What about me? Ain't I one of the leaders?"

"Yes," answered Tony quietly. "And I didn't ask you to do the job yourself. But I want you to handle it, to get the dope about where and when he can be put on a spot and then *get him.* You can work it your own way, have any of the boys you want to help you, but I want it *done."*

"And if I don't care to do it?" queried Steve impudently.

"You're through with this mob," retorted Tony coldly.

"After the orders Johnny left?"

"That don't cut any ice. There's nobody stays in this mob a minute that don't obey my orders. That goes for you as well as the truck drivers. And *there's* my authority!"

He whipped out his heavy, ugly automatic and slammed it down on the desk. Libati's glance riveted to the gun for a moment, then he looked up at Tony and his eyes shifted again. He rose.

"All right, I'll do it," he said, and walked out.

Tony smiled a little when the man had gone. Again he had won over the sullenly defiant Libati. He felt that he might yet master the fellow and make him a highly useful subordinate. Well, one thing certain; he'd either master him or make use of the authority he had exhibited to clinch his argument.

For half an hour Tony sat quietly smoking while he thought over the situation. It began to look as if this Schemer Bruno had come by his name rightfully, as if he were a worthy foe. And as an instrument with which to carry out his schemes he had as powerful a gang as was to be found in the United States. Its personnel was at least as strong as that of the Lovo mob and had proved itself to be equally resourceful and ruthless. And under the able leadership of this Schemer Bruno it seemed to have set out on the same sort of ambitious program of expansion that Tony himself now intended embarking upon with the aid of the Lovo gang.

Tony had heard, too, that the three most important gangs on the South Side were about to consolidate and, under a unified direction, attempt to extend their operations to the rest of the city. That meant three major organizations, each holding sovereignty over a certain section but struggling to gain the territory controlled by the others. It was going to be a grand fight, and a bloody one, with the big profits going to the gang that could shoot the straightest and whose leader could think the fastest. And Tony welcomed the coming battle, every wily, murderous phase of it.

He reached under the desk suddenly and, pressing a button there, summoned Al, the little, rat-faced gangster who acted as office boy and outer doorkeeper.

"I want somebody to do something for me," he said. "See who's downstairs and let me know right away."

In five minutes Al was back, and recited a list of the gangsters who were loafing in the cigar store below. Tony considered a moment.

"Tell Mike Rinaldo to come up here," he ordered finally.

Mike proved to be a slender, dark young man, foppishly dressed in the latest fashion, and with a somewhat elegant manner. In evening clothes, he could have passed as a foreign nobleman at a Ritz reception. Yet he was chief of the Lovo gang's gunmen and personally was the most daring and resourceful gunman Tony had ever encountered.

"Sit down, Mike," said Tony. "I've got a little job for you."

Mike obeyed, carefully easing his pants over his knees so as not to spoil their razor-like creases. Then he lighted an imported, cork-tipped cigarette with an ornate silver and mother-of-pearl lighter, and looked up expectantly.

"Do you know any of the men in the North Side mob?" demanded Tony.

"A few—by sight," answered Rinaldo, cautiously; his eyes narrowed with suspicion at the unusual question.

"I want one of 'em. And you're to get him for me."

"I don't think I quite get you, chief."

"I want one of Schemer Bruno's men—the higher up in the gang he is, the better I'll like it—brought here to me. I don't care how you do it just so he's alive when you get him here. I want to find out some details about how that mob operates."

"But, good God, chief, none of them would talk."

"The hell they wouldn't!" snapped Tony. "Did you ever see that little room we've got down in the cellar here?"

"No," answered Rinaldo, suddenly pale. "But I've heard about it."

"Oh, he'll talk all right," said Tony with a grim smile. "All you have to do is get him here. And if you get me somebody that knows something, there'll be five G's in it for you."

The gunman departed, his close-set eyes sparkling at the thought of making five hundred dollars in one chunk.

It was now after one in the morning. Tony could think of no other important tasks which could be done that night and decided to go home.

Jane Conley, famous in the underworld of half a dozen cities as "The Gun Girl," was still waiting up for him in the luxurious living room of the expensive apartment he had rented for the thirty-day period of unconventional trial marriage to which they had agreed. And he felt a quick surge of passion rush through him as his keen glance caught a suggestion of the alluring curves of her fine figure through the filmy folds of the flaming orange-and-black negligee which set off so brilliantly her vivid dark beauty.

A magazine lay open in her lap but her eyes looked red and strained, as if she might have been weeping.

"What's the matter, dear?" he asked after he had kissed her. "Unhappy already?"

She shook her head.

"I've been thinking. And I guess it kinda got me upset. You know, Tony, you ought to watch yourself more. Now that you're in Johnny Lovo's shoes, all these other mobs are going to try to bump you off. You ought to have bodyguards with you all the time."

"Yeah, I guess you're right, kid. I'll see about that tomorrow."

"And I think we ought to be better armed here."

"All right. I'll bring up a machine gun tomorrow night if you say so. Nobody knows we're here and if they did, they've got sense enough not to try to pull off anything in a place like this."

"You can't tell, Tony. All the mobs are getting too ambitious and from now it's going to be for blood."

"What's the matter; losin' your nerve?"

"Not by a damned sight!" flared Jane, her eyes snapping. "You know damn well I'm not yellow; I've proved it more than once. But I think it's foolish to take any more chances than you have to." She came to him impulsively and laid a hand on his arm. "I—I've got some things on my mind/ Tony, and if anything ever happened to you, I could never forgive myself."

With the taciturnity and inarticulateness of his kind, Tony did not question her about that cryptic remark. But to himself he puzzled over it. And before long he was destined to puzzle over it a lot more.

chapter 13

Tony read the newspapers next morning with unusual interest and a mounting fury. *GANG LEADER FLEES* was the big, black headline on all of them. Beneath that was a chronicle of Johnny Lovo's abdication and departure and of the succession of Tony Camonte, a young, little known gangster to his place as commander of the mob. And all the papers carried an interview with Captain Flanagan, chief of detectives, in which he calmly assumed credit for having run Lovo out of the city. The captain also intimated in the interview that the Lovo mob had been so thoroughly harassed by the men in his department that it was completely disorganized and would soon be a thing of the past. The captain closed with a trite, high-sounding but really meaningless statement as to the inevitable triumph of law and order when properly administered and promised the people that he would continue to exert his utmost efforts to rid the city of gangs. It was easy to see where the papers had received their information; the temptation to grab unearned glory had been too much for the captain.

"That bastard." Tony's voice crackled with venom as he spat out the epithet between clenched teeth. "I'll get him yet."

Tony drove to his headquarters with a ferocity that brought down upon him the profane maledictions of innumerable pedestrians and other motorists. But by the time he reached his desk his fury had cooled to an icy, wordless anger infinitely more dangerous. Never yet had he failed to get even with a betrayer.

"The D.A.'s been callin' up every five minutes for the last hour," said Al, the little, rat-faced doorman. "Said you was to give him a ring the minute you come in. Sounds like he's awful upset about somep'm."

"To hell with him!" snarled Tony. "If he wants to talk to me, he knows where to find me. We ought to get some service out of that bit we pay him every month."

"Better be careful with him, chief," warned Al. "He's more dangerous than any mob leader in town: He's got a strong-arm squad that's took many a poor guy for a ride."

Tony considered a moment then, with an angry grunt, reached for the telephone and called the District Attorney's office. At last there came to him over the wire a gruff voice that he recognized from that conference long ago to which he had accompanied Johnny Lovo.

"Camonte?" barked this voice brusquely. "This is District Attorney Crowder. I see in the morning papers that Lovo's left town."

"Yeah."

"And that you're in command of his mob now."

"Yeah, that's right."

"Well, I presume you are familiar with his — er — arrangement with me?"

"Yeah, I got a complete pay-off list of the bits and I'll keep takin' care of 'em just as he did."

"Don't say things like, that over the phone," commanded the D.A. sharply, in his voice such concern that Tony grinned. "Then things are going to go right ahead?"

"Yeah, only more so. This mob's been too quiet lately."

"Well, keep things out of the papers."

"That'd be easy, if the dicks wasn't so damn mouthy."

"I know. All right, then, I'll send Moran out to see you tomorrow afternoon."

Tony hung up, his lips curved in a sneering smile. The D.A. had been worried about his monthly bit, now that Lovo had gone. And he was sending Moran out for it the next afternoon. Moran was one of his younger assistants, a brilliant prosecutor when he and his chief wanted him to be, but in the meantime the collector for his superior.

Reporters besieged the headquarters all morning but Tony refused to see them or even to send out a statement. The less publicity he got, the better he liked it.

Shortly before noon Al brought in a note to him. It was written on cheap white paper in a graceful feminine hand and read:

Dear Mr. Camonte: —
May I see you for five minutes? Thanks!
Katherine Merton

Tony looked up, frowning in annoyance.

"Who's this dame?" he demanded.

"Don't know, chief. Never saw her before. But she sure is a swell looker."

"Yeah?" Tony seemed to brighten up a bit. "She don't look like a gun girl or anything?"

"Naw. A dame with eyes like this one's got couldn't hurt a kitten."

"All right, I'll take a chance. Send her in."

A moment later Miss Merton came in and Tony's first glimpse of her made him glad that he had granted the interview. Al's description of "a swell looker" was all right as far as it went but it did not take into account her dignity and charm. She was the sort of girl that immediately and unconsciously made a young man ambitious for more intimate acquaintance and an old man regretful for his age. Tall, with an athletic figure and an easy, graceful stride, she walked into the office with a calm, unbrazen assurance. She was dressed in a gray tweed suit and a small gray and black hat that fitted closely the fine contour of her head.

"How do you do, Mr. Camonte," she said, and extended her hand. "I'm Miss Merton."

Tony accepted the hand and felt sorry that he had no right or excuse for holding it longer than he did. Her voice was rich and soothing, well-placed and completely poised, and her frank blue eyes held an engaging twinkle of understanding good humor.

"I want to ask a favor of you, Mr. Camonte," she began. "I've found that men of your type are almost always chivalrous if they have the opportunity to be."

"Yeah, sure," mumbled Tony, embarrassed. "Be glad to do anything I can."

"I thought so. Now, the problem is this: I have a job that I very much want to keep. And right now you are the only person in the city who can help me keep that job."

"Yeah? How's that?"

"I'm with the *Examiner,*" continued the girl gently, almost regretfully. "And the city editor told me this morning that if I didn't succeed in getting an interview with you he'd fire me."

"A reporter!" exclaimed Tony in amazement and his expressive black eyes flashed angrily. "I'm not seeing any reporters."

"I knew you wouldn't, of course. And I understand just how you feel. But you see how it was with me—I *had* to come out here and try to see you or lose my job. I guess, though, that I'll lose it anyway."

She sighed and, succeeding in looking small and miserable for a moment, sniffed audibly. Tony growled under his breath and lit a cigarette.

"Well, miss, I can't tell anything about my business," he objected doggedly.

"Of *course* you can't." She seemed amazed at the mere idea. "And I wouldn't think of asking you anything like that, even to save my job. All I wanted to know was if Mr. Lovo really had left and if you really were going to be the commander from now on—my, I should think it would require unlimited brains and nerve to manage an—er—operation like this. And you look so young to have such an important position."

During the ensuing twenty minutes Miss Merton secured her interview. Her questions were adroitly harmless on the surface, dealing only with things which were already known or soon would be known about the gang and its operations, and Tony had no realization of how much he had said.

"I'll bet you'd make a wonderful husband," she said finally, her eyes sparkling in a way that gave him an unaccountable thrill. "Men who lead adventurous lives always do; they like the relief of a quiet, comfortable home."

Thus she steered the conversation into romantic channels and for some little time they dealt with love, marriage and so on. Mostly they talked in generalities but occasionally she elicited from him a personal opinion that would be meat for a sensational newspaper story on "A Gang Leader's Ideas of Love" or some such shop-girl-appeal topic.

"By the way," she said at last, "did you ever know a girl named Vyvyan Lovejoy?"

The question gave Tony such a shock that he almost cried out. Only his iron reserve enabled him to keep from betraying himself by an obvious reaction. Did he know Vyvyan Lovejoy? Did Romeo know Juliet? Vyvyan was the burlesque leading woman who had been his first love. He had killed Al Spingola, the city's most important gang leader at that time, in order that he might have her for himself. It was his reckless love for her that had started him on his career beyond the law. And when he had come back from the war and found her living with another man he had killed them both. At the mention of her name, all these events had rushed through his mind like a private mental movie. As it came to an end, his eyes narrowed and his mouth set grimly.

"No," he said. "Why do you ask?"

"I interviewed her once," answered the girl smoothly. "And you look a great deal like a picture she had. There's something about the eyes— "

Tony felt considerably upset. To his knowledge, Vyvyan had never had a picture of him. Nor had anyone else. In fact, he didn't know of his picture ever having been taken. He didn't believe in pictures; they were too liable to fall into the wrong hands and some time be a means of identification.

"And by the way," continued Miss Merton smoothly, "do you ever see that stunning brunette who was with you at the Embassy Club the night Jerry Hoffman was shot?"

At this question, Tony did start. Even his iron-like nerves could not withstand a shock like that. He and Jane Conley, "The Gun Girl," the girl with whom he was now living, had killed Jerry Hoffman, then leader of the North Side gang, that night at the Embassy Club, the city's most exclusive night resort. Johnny Lovo had given the orders and paid for the job being done. And so far as Tony knew, Lovo was the only other person besides himself and Jane who even knew that they had been in the club that fatal night.

"I don't know what you're talking about," he said.

"You see, I was there that night and my escort pointed out all the notables to me. You were among them. He said he thought you would make a great success in your chosen profession." She laughed lightly.

"Who was your escort that night?" demanded Tony.

"Oh, I don't think it would be fair to tell." She rose, smilingly, and extended her hand. "I won't take up any more of your valuable time now, Mr. Camonte. But perhaps some other time we can chat a bit. Anyway, thanks so much for a very interesting interview; it will enable me to keep my job."

And she departed, leaving behind her a much perturbed gang leader. Now that he was no longer under the influence of her personality—and her expert flattery —he realized that she was a smooth worker, that she had attained her objective in spite of him. And how had she known so much? And what could possibly have been her object in mentioning those past occurrences to him?

The more he thought about it the more worried he became. At last, in response to a sudden awful suspicion, he picked up the telephone and, calling the *Examiner,* asked to speak to Miss Katherine Merton. A moment later he hung up slowly, feeling dazed and very uneasy. *The Examiner had no one by that name.* Then who was the girl? And what had been her object?

chapter 14

Charlie Martino, the alky truck driver, who had been hijacked and shot the, night before, died during the afternoon, without regaining sufficient strength to relate the details of what had occurred to him or to give a description of his assailants. Tony looked down at the boy a moment, then, using again that uncanny yet unconscious knowledge of psychology which he possessed, ordered every member of the gang who could be reached to come in a few at a time and view the body. He felt that the sight of one of their own dead would put the spirit of battle in them. At last he ordered a fine funeral for the boy and went back to his private office in grim silence, vowing vengeance on the North Side gang.

Tony, in a savage humor from the day's events, was just ready to go home shortly after ten that night when Mike Rinaldo, the dapper gunman, arrived. And the three men who followed him into Tony's office proved that he had succeeded in his quest. For the man in the center was obviously a prisoner.

"Got him, chief," announced Mike with an elegant gesture toward the glowering captive.

"Who is he?" demanded Tony. His manner indicated that nothing short of Caesar himself would be acceptable.

"Benny Peluso, one of the big shots in the North Side crowd."

"Frisk him?"

"Certainly," answered Rinaldo, evidently aggrieved at the query. "Found a nice load of gats too."

"Well, frisk him again here. Strip him to the hide."

From his vantage point behind the big desk Tony surveyed the captive while his three henchmen stripped the man and searched every inch of his clothing for possible weapons. The fellow was short and slightly stocky, with a heavy brutal face that instantly bred distrust. His black eyes, now blazing with anger, were shifty and set far too close together.

Tony removed a heavy automatic from the desk drawer and laid it on the desk conveniently close to his practiced right hand.

"All right," he said when the three men had completed their fruitless search and the prisoner was indignantly donning his coat. "You," pointing the pistol at the captive, "sit down there. The rest of you wait outside until I call you."

He toyed silently with the weapon until the door had closed behind his men. Then he looked at Peluso and stared at him until the man's glance dropped.

"Do you know where you are?" demanded Tony suddenly.

"Yeah," snarled the prisoner.

"Speak nicer if you expect to get out of here alive," snapped Tony. "Do you know who I am?"

"No."

"Well, I'm Scarface Tony Camonte, the new chief of the Lovo mob. And I'm just about ten times as hard-boiled as Johnny Lovo ever thought of bein'. I've bumped off six or eight myself and another one—especially a rat like you—wouldn't mean a thing in my young life. Get me?"

"Yeah." But the man's tone now had changed from defiant anger to sullenness and his glance remained riveted hypnotically to that pistol.

"There's some things I want to know. And *you're* goin' to tell me."

"You got the wrong man, brother. I won't spill nothin'."

"The *hell* you won't!" Tony leaned across the desk, the pistol pointed unwaveringly at the hapless captive. "Do you want a load of that in you?"

"Naw, course not. But if I talked, my own crowd would bump me off."

"Maybe not." Tony leaned back. "How much jack do you make with your mob?"

"'Bout three C's a week. Sometimes more."

"Three C's, eh? That's not very much, is it, for all the work you do and the chances you take?"

"I'm wort' more," agreed the man darkly.

"Yeah. But you'll never get it, not with this Bruno guy, from what I hear of him. Where do you think he got that name *Schemer* anyhow? When a guy has a monicker like that hung on him there's a reason for it. Now, Benny, I'm not a bad guy when you don't cross me. And I'm always willing to see the boys get a piece of change for themselves." He leaned across the desk. "How would you like to have fifteen grand—in one chunk?"

The prisoner's eyes sparkled and he licked his lips.

"Jeez!" he exclaimed. "Dat's a lotta jack, even if y'ain't got it."

"I've got it. And it's yours if you want to talk."

"What do you want to know?"

"That's more like it," smiled Tony. "I want to know a lot of things about the Bruno mob, where their warehouses are, and their breweries and their main alky cooking plants. I want to know what garages they keep their trucks in and what roads they use mainly in haulin' their stuff in and out of town. I'll think of a few more things as we go along."

"God! I couldn't tell you all dat stuff."

"Why not?"

"Dey'd bump me off sure."

"Well, if you don't tell me what I want to know, *I'll* bump you off."

"An' if I do tell you, dey will. What chance has a poor guy got?"

"Listen, mug!" snapped Tony. "Don't you know that fifteen grand's a lot of dough? That's as much as you make in a year with the mob, and if you stay here with them you'll never have that much in one chunk. If you had that much jack, you could go to Frisco or New York or even Mexico or some other crazy place and open a gambling house or get in some kind of a racket and be set for life."

"Yeah, I know. I—I'd like to have it all right. But dem guys would follow me *any* place."

"They wouldn't know where you was. They'd think you'd been took for a ride. Don't plenty of mugs from these mobs around here disappear every year?"

"Yeah, I guess they do. But I couldn't do it. They'd get me sure. And what good's dough to a dead man?"

"Come on, now, don't be a fool!" snarled Tony menacingly and aimed the pistol again. "Either you talk or you get it."

The man's eyes glittered against the background of his ghastly pale face and he licked his lips constantly.

"Well, I know I'm goin' to get it if I do talk," he answered doggedly. "So I guess I'll have to take my chances of gettin' it if I don't."

"So you won't spill it, eh?" gritted Tony.

The hole in the muzzle of that automatic must have looked as big as a barrel to the prisoner. But he caught his breath suddenly, closed his eyes and shook his head.

"I think you will!" said Tony. "Get up!"

He called in his henchmen from the other room.

"He's a hard nut," he explained. "Got to take him to the cellar."

Rinaldo paled. He could shoot a man down without even giving serious thought to the matter but the mere thought of what was in that cellar made him weak.

"Come on!" snapped Tony and included them all with a comprehensive gesture of the automatic.

"Ya takin' me for a ride?" asked the prisoner as they descended in the elevator.

"No," retorted Tony grimly. "Not yet."

The place to which they took him was a subcellar beneath the regular cellar under the hotel. It was reached by a rather rickety wooden stairway and proved to be a large square room with concrete walls from which were suspended by chains various strange-looking iron appendages. Before Peluso could hardly realize what was happening he had been stripped to the waist and rigged up against the wall, his arms stretched high overhead, his body suspended from the wrists which were encircled by tight iron bands. Tony motioned to one of his men who stepped over to a small, furnace-like arrangement. Tony himself caught up a large, razor-edged knife and, fingering it significantly, looked at his prisoner.

"You know, Benny," he said grimly, "a lot of these mugs they find out on the road somewhere after they've been took for a ride don't look so pretty; ears off, tongue out, and other little details like that. *And all those things always happen before the guy is actually bumped off.* Nice to think about, ain't it?"

Tony turned back toward the furnace. Rinaldo followed him.

"I don't like to say nothin', chief," said the gunman hoarsely in a low tone, "but, honest to God, I don't believe I can stand this."

"Then look the other way or get out. I don't like it any better than you do but it's got to be done. Makin' this bird talk means that our mob will control the city before long. And don't forget this, Mike; Bruno or any of that North Side mob of his would do this same thing to you or me or any of us in a minute if they had the chance." He turned abruptly to the other man. "Ready?" he demanded brusquely.

"Here you are, chief."

From within the furnace, the gangster drew out a long, thin iron bar. One end of it was red hot. Tony caught it up by the cold end and approached the trussed prisoner.

"Now, damn you," he snarled, "you'll either talk or I'll ram a hole clear through you with this."

And he started the sizzling iron bar slowly but surely toward the gangster's bare flesh. The man cringed and his eyes widened with terror. Finally he yelled, though the iron had not yet touched him.

"Go ahead and yell," said Tony grimly. "Nobody'll hear you."

Facing a pistol is one thing; facing red hot iron against one's bare flesh and other unknown tortures is another. Peluso cracked.

"I'll talk! I'll talk! I'll talk!" he gibbered when the iron was yet half an inch from him. "God! take that away."

For an hour they cross-examined him, Rinaldo and the others jotting down details while Tony asked the questions. The leader's eyes were sparkling; he was gaining a complete knowledge of the operations of his most important enemy.

"Well, do I get the dough?" asked Peluso when he finally had convinced them that he knew no more.

"Yes," retorted Tony. "After we've checked up on this story of yours and carried out a plan or two I'm hatching up right now. In the meantime, you stay *here;* I'm not takin' any chances with you rushin' to Bruno and blabbin' everything to him so that he could change his whole line-up before I can ruin it for him."

Tony immediately selected his half dozen cleverest men—including Mike Rinaldo—and sent them out to investigate what Peluso had told. For over a week they worked day and night, circulating around the city, spying, asking apparently aimless questions, doing a great deal of motoring, snooping carefully but efficiently in many quarters. And they reported back that every detail of the prisoner's story seemed correct.

Elated, Tony at once set in motion the machinery over which he now had control. A dozen new machine guns were imported from New York by devious methods. And certain members of the gang who were acknowledged experts in that line were set to work constructing powerful bombs, or "pineapples" as they are known in gang circles. Tony was a veritable dynamo of energy during these preparations and his vigorous—and murderous—enthusiasm gradually communicated itself to the others until the entire gang was a real fighting machine anxious to get a chance at the enemy.

Libati came swaggering into Tony's private office, late one afternoon.

"Well, I guess we're about all ready for the war to start. What's the first move?"

"I'll let you know when I've decided," retorted Tony coolly.

"How about this mug, Peluso? What are we goin' to do with him?"

"Do with him! Why, as soon as the campaign on the North Side gang is well opened up, I'm goin' to give him the jack I promised him and have him taken to a train for the West. I imagine he'll be glad enough to blow town."

"I'd think so. But surely you're not goin' to be such a sap as to pay him off now. He's told us all he knows. Why not take him for a ride and save the dough?"

Tony, unaccountably shocked by the cold-blooded proposal, looked up with flashing eyes.

"I keep my word, Steve, whether to friend or enemy, and no matter what I've promised, either good or bad," he retorted grimly. "The other day I gave you an assignment to get a certain man. You haven't done it yet. Do you remember what I promised you if you didn't carry it out?"

Steve's glance shifted uneasily. "Yes."

"Well, that stands. And I don't intend to wait all summer either. Better get a move on."

chapter 15

Tony took Jane Conley, "The Gun Girl," to one of the swankier night resorts that evening. They both enjoyed such high-powered diversion and it always brought back memories. It was at Ike Bloom's that Tony first had seen her and been struck by her beauty. It was at the Embassy Club, while they sat waiting for Jerry Hoffman to come in so that they could carry out he death sentence pronounced on him by their employer, Johnny Lovo, that they really had become acquainted.

Tony, his evening clothes immaculate and perfectly fitted save for a slight bulge under his left arm where an automatic hung suspended in a shoulder holster, looked about the luxurious but crowded and noisy place, then glanced at Jane with satisfaction glowing in his expressive eyes. She was the most beautiful woman in the place, or the "joint," as he mentally worded it. He wondered, with a sudden twinge of jealousy, if she would stick with him after the thirty-day probationary period had expired.

He observed that she seemed somewhat distraught tonight, her hands fluttered nervously, little lines of concern wrinkle her forehead, and her glance kept wandering around as though she were looking for somebody, yet hoping that she wouldn't see him.

"What'sa matter, baby?" asked Tony expansively.

"Nothing. I just don't feel very well."

"Aw, cheer up! Let's dance!"

They rose and moved out on the small, crowded floor, quite the handsomest couple in the place. Jane was a superb dancer and Tony, with his native Latin grace and sense of rhythm, equally good. Nobody watching them would have dreamed that they both had killed, not in the heat of passion, but coolly and deliberately— for money; and that they would kill again whenever the occasion seemed to demand. And yet they were not murderers, except legally. In their own minds, they felt completely justified for everything they had done. And their operation never had been and never would be the slightest menace to the general public. When they stalked with murderous intent, they invariably were after some certain person who had it coming to him and who would have done the same to them without any more compunction than they showed. And they always took care not to harm innocent bystanders.

When the cabaret's gaiety was at its height in the wee hours, Tony saw Katherine Merton, the mysterious girl who, in the guise of a newspaper reporter, had visited him at headquarters and questioned him at length about many things. She was seated now on the other side of the club, attired in a somewhat daring evening gown of flashing sequins, and escorted by a dark, handsome man in a dinner jacket, whose general appearance, somehow, was anything but reassuring to Tony.

He wondered suddenly why she was here, if there was anything behind her presence beyond participation in the general gaiety. The possibility worried him. He wondered if she had seen him, and hoped she had not.

"Say, baby," he said, "do you know that dame over there, the one with the diamond dress?"

Jane turned and her glance searched the room. When she finally saw the mysterious girl, her eyes widened and she bit her lip.

"No," she answered sharply. Then: "Let's go!"

Puzzled, Tony escorted her from the club. He knew she had lied. But why? Newsboys were crying the early editions of the morning papers. Tony bought one, then his face set and an involuntary "Hell!" burst from his lips.

"What's the matter?" asked Jane anxiously.

"Steve missed, the damn dumbbell!" snarled Tony.

The girl took the paper from him and looked at it. An attempt had been made that night on the life of Schemer Bruno, now leader of the North Side gang. But miraculously he had come through it unscathed. Questioned by police, he had admitted that he had an idea who was behind the attack but had refused to give them any information. It was thought by the police that the attack meant the beginning of a new gang war.

"The clumsy fool!" snarled Tony. "I should have known better than to trust that job to him. Now Bruno will be after us *right*. And he'll be so careful himself that we may not be able to get another crack at him for a hell of a while."

"Oh, Tony, that worries me!" said Jane. "You must be very careful."

He drove home in wordless wrath, his active mind racing with murderous plans for annihilating his enemies. In front of the luxurious apartment house where they lived he stopped and let Jane out.

"I'll put the car away and be right back," he said absently.

At the corner he swung to the left and headed for the garage a block away. Suddenly the angry whine of a heavy car approaching from the rear at high speed obtruded itself into his consciousness. Instantly suspicious, he increased his own speed. But the other car came alongside. He could see that it was long and low and black, with side-curtains in place—the typical death car. Then a thin red stream burst from its side, he heard the rattle of machine-gun fire, and bullets tattooed against the side of his own car. But the body of his sedan was heavy steel and the glass was bullet-proof. It shed bullets as a duck does water. Yet these enemies, whoever they were, would not be satisfied until they had accomplished their murderous mission.

He realized that he dare not go into the garage for the death car would follow and finish him there. And: the employees would be of no help. He must get to his own district, where these men would hardly dare follow and where, if they did, his gangsters always loafing around that all-night cigar store on the ground floor of the hotel which was his headquarters would come to his assistance and make short work of them.

Abruptly he pressed the accelerator to the floor and the big car leaped forward. At a crazy pace he raced through the dark, deserted city streets. And that other car hung doggedly to his trail. Several times they gained slightly, coming almost close enough to use their guns again. But always he managed to keep ahead of them.

On and on and on went that strange race, for him a race for life, for them a race for death—his death; careening around corners, streaking along on the straightaway. If only he could reach his headquarters before something happened. Surely they would not dare to follow him there.

From behind came the stuttering rat-tat-tat of machine-gun fire again. Two of his tires, evidently pierced by the bullets, blew out with loud reports. The car slewed to the right, struck the curb with

terrific force, and turned over. Tony felt himself falling then everything went black.

When he regained consciousness he was lying prone but in an
uncomfortably cramped position. There was a carpet under him and
feet all around him and he was aware of a jolting, swaying motion.
Abruptly he realized that he was on the floor of a car tonneau and
that the car was moving. It couldn't be his car. Then it must be that
of the enemy. He sat up, wildly staring about him. There were two
men in the rear seat but it was too ark to distinguish their faces.

"He ain't dead, after all," said a strange voice. "Jeez! ain't that top
bad?"

"What the hell's the idea?" demanded Tony.

"You'll know soon enough."

"Well, let me up on the seat there. This is too damned uncomfortable."

He tried to get up and found that he was weak and very dizzy. One
of the men reached out and jerked him into the seat between them.
He could see now that the front seat also contained two men.

"You want to enjoy this ride, kid!" snarled a voice in his ear.
"Because it's the last one you'll ever take."

Tony's heart almost stopped. He'd faced danger and been in tight
places before; but never a situation like this. He was being taken for
a ride, about to be made the victim of the most feared and the most
conclusive of all the means gangland used for ridding itself of its
enemies. He turned to the man who had spoken.

"This is some of that damn crooked North Side outfit, I suppose,"
he said bitterly.

"Yes."

"Who the hell are you?"

"Me?" The man laughed mirthlessly, a menacing laugh strangely
like the rattling of a snake about to strike. "I'm Jerry Hoffman's
brother."

chapter 16

Mentally Tony rehearsed the steps ahead of him. The swift, ominously silent ride out into the country. Then when a sufficiently
deserted spot had been reached, he would be kicked out of the car,
riddled with bullets and left dead in a ditch, to be found by some
passerby or perhaps picked to pieces by buzzards if the place were
remote enough.

A fellow had some chance in a street gun-fight, no matter what the odds against him, but a ride was more inexorable than the death sentence imposed by a jury and court. For there was no appeal from it. There was no possibility of escape from it. It was carried out with the cool, precise deadliness of a state execution. And it was even more inevitable—at least it always had been.

A nervous or . sensitive man, faced with cruel, and certain death within an hour, would have shouted, screamed, pleaded, perhaps battled his captors with that reckless strength born of despair. But Tony was neither nervous nor sensitive. A man who requires a steady trigger finger can't be. Tony was thinking. Not with frantic, chaotic haste; but coldly, deliberately, resourcefully.

The hopelessness of his situation did not appall him. It merely stimulated that abnormally keen animal cunning which had made him, while still in the twenties, the most daring and powerful gang leader in that city noted for daring and powerful gang leaders.

And at last his agile mind found a possibility— focused upon it. It was a mad scheme; the chances were a hundred to one against his coming out of it alive even if it worked. He realized that, yet experience had taught him that a plan seemingly impossible of success sometimes succeeded because people thought nobody would be silly enough to try it. As things stood, he was sure to be dead within an hour; if he attempted his mad plan, he had a bare chance. He decided without a second thought to assume the risk.

Calmly, coolly, he bided his time, sitting there in the tonneau of the big car between two of his captors while the other two occupied the front seat. At last he saw a car approaching from the other direction. His gaze narrowed as he tried to gauge their relative speeds and the distance between them.

Then, with a sudden, panther-like spring, he leaped forward, launching a terrific blow at the chauffeur's head and grabbing for the wheel. The speeding car staggered crazily. But the surprised driver was still hanging on. Tony was battering the man's head, trying to strangle him, with one hand while he tugged at the wheel with the other. He felt blows raining on his own head and back, then a gun flashed and roared in the tonneau and he felt a sharp burning in his side. But he gritted his teeth and stuck to his task.

The big car swerved to the right, dropped into the ditch with a blinding crash, then turned over and over, its engine racing madly with a shrill, agonized whine, and finally came to rest on its side, still quivering, like a stricken animal.

Tony piled on top of the other two men who had been with him in the tonneau, shook his whirling head in an effort to clear it. His whole body seemed to be only a mass of excruciating pains, but he was still conscious. He realized dully that none of the others had moved or spoken. His left arm was twisted under him in an unnatural way. He tried to move it and found he couldn't. It was hurting terribly, too. Cautiously he reached out with his right hand, feeling the pockets of his inert companions. Finding a familiar bulge, he reached in and pulled out a .45 automatic.

The feel of the cold steel against his flesh, the realisation that he was armed again, revived him like cold water. He struggled upward, seeking a way out of the twisted wreckage. Then he heard approaching footsteps clicking on the frozen ground and a shadowy figure appeared beside the overturned car. That was somebody from the other automobile, of course; he had counted on that.

"Say!" he said hoarsely, and was provoked to find his voice shaky. "Help me out of here, will you?"

A flashlight was snapped on, then its conic yellow beam penetrated the tonneau and finally came to rest on his face.

"Sure!" said the stranger. "But I'm surprised any of you are alive. God! That was an awful sight!"

He helped Tony out through a smashed and twisted door, then turned his light on the others. The driver and his companion were obviously dead, their faces horribly cut by the broken glass. The two men in the tonneau were unconscious but looked to be alive.

"Come on, let's go," said Tony.

"But the others—" objected the stranger in amazement.

"To hell with the others!" snarled Tony harshly. "They're gangsters and they was takin' me for a ride. I hope they're all dead. I guess I ought to make sure—"

He produced the pistol and aimed at the two inert figures in the tonneau.

"For God's sake!" gasped the stranger, laying a trembling hand on his arm. "Don't! You can't—"

Tony turned and stared at him for a moment, then shrugged contemptuously and allowed his gun hand to drop to his side. He had decided that it would probably be best not to do any murdering before a witness, especially when he needed that witness badly for the next half hour.

"All right!" he growled. "But you're goin' to take me where I want to go, and take me fast. Come on!"

He prodded the stranger with the automatic then almost grinned as the man shivered and hastily began leading the way back to his own car parked on the road.

Tony ordered the man to make all speed for the gang's headquarters then silently settled back in the seat with a sigh of relief and began making plans for vengeance. But his own misery would not allow his mind to dwell on that enticing problem. His left arm was broken; his right side throbbed and burned from the bullet wound; he found it impossible to assume a position which was even remotely comfortable. And pain and warm little trickles warned him that his own face had not escaped the flying glass. Altogether he felt, and imagined that he looked, a total wreck.

The man beside him obviously was burning up with curiosity. Several times he tried to question his passenger but Tony either answered in grunts or not at all and he finally gave it up. But he drove like fury; they pulled up before the hotel gang headquarters, much sooner than Tony expected.

"You're all right," said the gang leader briefly, reaching for his wallet. He found it contained three hundred and forty dollars and generously thrust the whole wad of bills into the surprised stranger's still trembling hand. "There's a little gas money," he said with an attempt at a smile. Then his face sobered into a frown and his voice came hoarsely from between gritted teeth. "But keep your mouth shut about this!" he commanded savagely. "Or you'll get what they tried to give me tonight."

Even at that hour of the morning, there were a few gangsters lounging in the all-night cigar store and in the small, dark lobby of the hotel. Tony's entrance in such a condition created a sensation and they all looked eagerly curious.

"Been in an automobile wreck," volunteered Tony curtly, then immediately ascended to his own private quarters on the top floor and called a doctor.

An hour later, his wounds dressed and his broken arm set, Tony went to bed. He felt certain he would be unable to sleep, yet it was after noon when he awakened. Laboriously he hauled his weary, battered frame out of bed and tried to dress. But with only one arm, and it so stiff and sore that he could hardly move it, he had to call Al, the little, rat-faced doorkeeper to help him.

Fortunately Tony kept part of his extensive wardrobe at the hotel; he would have looked funny transacting the day's business in evening dress. He had a big breakfast sent up then went to his desk and sent for Steve Libati. And his eyes flashed as he gave the order. This was to be a day of settling scores.

chapter 17

The assistant chief of the powerful Lovo gang came in with an air of genial assurance that somehow seemed forced. His ugly face bore a smile but his eyes were narrowed and searching, as if he were anxious to know what sort of reception he was to receive.

"Sorry to hear about your accident, boss," he said. "The cops phoned that your car had been found out on the North Side some-where. There's been a lot of reporters out here this morning, too; they say there's bullet-holes in the tires. But I told 'em you wasn't around—"

"Yeah," growled Tony sourly, "you're a big help to me." He stiff-ened and leaned across the desk, his mouth twisted in an ugly snarl. "What the hell did you miss Bruno for?" he demanded.

Libati shrugged. "Just a rotten break."

"What do you mean—a rotten break?" demanded Tony savagely. "Bullets go where they're aimed.... How'd you try to pull the job, anyway?"

Libati explained. One of the two gunmen that he had selected to help him murder Schemer Bruno, wily leader of the strong North Side gang, had discovered that Bruno was to visit a certain place at ten o'clock the night before. In a parked car across the street, they had lain in wait for him. He came out in a few minutes and just as they were ready to fire, another car had run through the street, obscuring their human target for a moment. When their opportuni-ty finally came, he was walking rapidly toward his car. They had all fired a volley at him and then fled in their car, before his friends inside the saloon could pile out and make the gun fight two-sided.

"All three of you put a rod on him?" demanded Tony.

"Yeah."

"And all three of you missed?"

"I—guess so. The papers this morning says he wasn't hit by this 'mysterious attack'!"

"Well, what a fine lot of gat-packers you are," snarled Tony in disgust. "Why, I could throw a gat at a guy and hit him with it.... Why in hell didn't you finish the job?"

"But them guys inside—"

"If there's anything I hate, it's a quitter.... I s'pose you didn't know that if you missed, Bruno was sure to know who was behind the attack and set all his gorillas on *my* trail.... Listen, Steve, there's two kinds of guys that this mob ain't big enough to hold—those that can't obey orders and those that won't obey orders. And I think both counts fit you."

Libati flushed slowly until his swarthy complexion had turned a sort of dull purple. And his shifty black eyes had taken on a glittering menace.

"I—don't think I get you," he said slowly, and his lips compressed into a thin, hard line.

"No? Well, I'll put it plainer, so plain that even *you* can get it. Either you and the men you picked to help you get Bruno are no good or you sold out to the enemy and missed on purpose."

"Damn you!" gritted Libati, leaping to his feet, his right hand darting for his side coat pocket.

But Tony, with the smooth ease and incredible rapidity of the expert, had lifted his automatic from the desk and had it trained on his lieutenant's middle coat button before the man was completely out of the chair.

"Don't pull, you fool!" hissed the leader. "I don't weaken and I don't miss. And you better not let that right mitt of yours get nervous again while you're in my presence. It's only my *left* arm that's broke, you know," he added with grim humor.

Steve let his gun hand fall to his side, then ostentatiously lifted it to light, a cigarette that he had taken from his left hand pocket.

"You've been after my job ever since Johnny left," said Tony. "And you ain't the type to be particular how you got it—or anything else, for that matter. If I was dead, you'd have it, see? That's why it would be so nice for *you* to have Schemer Bruno still alive so he could get me. Well, I ain't dead yet, Steve, and I don't intend to be for a long time. So I think you're wastin' your valuable time around here waitin' for me to drop off." His voice dropped to the cold, monotonous level of a judge pronouncing sentence. "You and those two mugs who was with you last night are through with this mob."

"Don't talk foolish!" snapped Steve. "You can't fire me out of this mob. Johnny—"

"Johnny's gone. And he left me the boss. There's my " authority," lifting, the heavy automatic and gazing at it—fondly. "From today on you don't get a dime out of here and if I hear of you hangin' around here, it's liable to be curtains. You're all through, see? You can either go out like you are or in a hearse, I don't care which."

For a long moment the two men looked into each other's eyes. Tony's were cold, hard, steady; 'Steve's shifty and blazing with fury. Rut at last the erstwhile lieutenant turned without a word and strode out of the room. Again Tony had won; permanently this time, it seemed.

Tony's *next* act was to arrange a bodyguard for himself, an ample one. Then, with a retinue befitting a per—son of his importance— and danger—he returned to his apartment. From now on he would travel as he was doing now, between two watchful henchmen in the rear seat of a sedan with a steel body and bullet-proof glass while the well-armed chauffeur and the man beside him, as well as the four men following closely in a similar car maintained a constant vigil in every direction for suspicious automobiles or people.

Tony entered his luxurious apartment briskly, his hard eyes glinting with anger. There were a lot of things he wanted to ask Jane.

He found her curled up in a big chair in the living room, reading a novel and munching a box of chocolates with what he considered unpardonable placidness. She looked up in surprise at his entrance, then her eyes widened in shocked amazement as she noted his appearance.

"Why, Tony!" she exclaimed. "What's happened?"

"A lot you care!" he growled. "I go around the corner to put the car away and don't come back till the next day and you look as if you hadn't even wondered what kept me."

"But I *have* wondered, Tony. I've been terribly anxious. But I supposed that you knew your own business and I thought you might resent my butting into your affairs."

"Yeah? Well, the Bruno mob tried to take me for a ride last night. And I think you knew they were goin' to."

"Tony!" The girl's face had gone deathly white and her eyes were glittering. "How can you say—"

"Who was that dame at the cabaret last night, the good-lookin' moll in white with that dark mug in a dress suit?"

"I—I don't know."

"Yes, you do. I pointed her out to you and I could see in your eyes that you knew her." He went close to her, caught her arm in a vise-like grip and twisted cruelly. "Who was she?" he rasped.

"She's—a gun girl," panted Jane finally. "Schemer Bruno's moll."

"So *that's* it, eh?" He released Jane's arm and stepped back, gazing down at her with sneering contempt. "Was that Bruno with her?"

"Yes."

"God! If I'd only known that," gritted the gang leader, murder in his eyes. "And you knew it all the time and wouldn't tell me.?'

"No. If I had, you'd have tried to bump him off right there. And you would have either been killed by some of his mob—he always has a bodyguard with him—or been pinched by the cops and tried for the job."

"Humph! Don't make me laugh! They couldn't hang anything on me in this town."

"Don't be too sure! Bootlegging's one thing; murder's another."

"What made you want to leave right away when you saw her and Bruno?"

"I—was afraid they might be going to try to pull something. I wanted to get home—to get out of their reach."

"Humph! Looks to me like you were more afraid of your own hide than mine."

"What if I didn't want to get bumped off?" demanded the girl, a trace of her usual defiant assurance returning. "Nobody wants to croak at my age. But I was worried about you, too, Tony," she continued hurriedly as she saw the storm clouds gathering in his face. "Haven't I tried for days to make you fix a bodyguard for yourself?"

Tony considered, realizing the truth of that. She had pleaded with him for the past two weeks to arrange a competent bodyguard for himself. But he had hesitated, feeling that to move around constantly surrounded by a squad of gunmen was a reflection upon his own courage and marksmanship. Yet he could not rid himself entirely of the idea that she had been treacherous to him. And his ruthless direct mind could find only penalty for treachery—Death.

"I love you, Tony," she went on while his piercing glance surveyed her. "And I've been doing everything I could to protect you."

"Yeah? Well, I have my doubts. But I'll give you a chance to prove it. If you love me, get Schemer Bruno for me."

Her eyes widened slowly as she realized the enormity of the assignment and the thoughts within his mind that must have prompted it. Tony laughed.

"Lost your nerve?" he demanded.

Jane gazed at him with sudden contempt. "Of course not!" she snapped. "I've got as much guts as you—any day in the week, big shot."

"Yeah? Then prove it and your love for me by gettin' the Schemer."

"What a nice chivalrous mugg you turned out to be!" she rasped contemptuously. "Handing me the job of bumping off the biggest rod in town—next to you. And alone. You know damn well, Tony, that I never pulled a job by myself. But I'm quite a help, if you'll just remember back to the time that we got Jerry Hoffman together that night in the Embassy Club. But if you'll help, I'll do my part. I'll snoop around until I find when he'll be on a spot. Then we'll pull the job together."

"Well, all right," he growled. He had cooled off considerably from his first anger and as he surveyed the girl's ample charms, but illy concealed by an expensive negligee, he decided that it probably would be best not to lose her just yet. But of course he must not let her realize that. He stepped forward and caught her arm again. "But you little devil;" he rasped through gritted teeth, "if I ever catch you turnin' me up or doin' me any kind of dirt, it'll be *curtains.* See?"

So these two, who never had failed to complete a killing assigned them, assigned one to themselves and verbally signed Schemer Bruno's death warrant. Yet Tony's doubts and the ensuing quarrel had opened in their relations a rift which was to have far-reaching consequences.

chapter 18

Tony immediately set out on a reckless yet precisely deadly campaign of reprisal against the North Side mob led by the redoubtable Schemer Bruno. He was beginning to have a sneaking respect for the notorious Schemer. He had seen plenty of examples of that wily leader's sagacity and ruthless courage and that business at the cabaret had been the final touch. A man who could, an hour after an attempt had been made on his life, sit in a cabaret but a few tables away from the man he knew to be responsible for that attempt, was a man worthy of admiration. But the realization of his opponent's courage and ability only strengthened Tony's will to win and forced him to plan out amazing coups.

They bombed warehouses, hijacked trucks both singly and in fleets, intimidated still-owners who helped supply the North Side outfit into moving and shot a few as an example to the others; browbeat saloonkeepers into shifting their allegiance and promised them ample protection for doing so; killed off half a dozen of Bruno's best gunmen and threatened others with the same fate if they didn't leave town; repeatedly held up and robbed gambling houses known to be owned by Bruno and bombed those that put in the speakeasy system of locked steel doors and peep-holes: and in general harassed the other gang in every way possible to a daringly resourceful leader and a powerful organization.

When his campaign was rolling merrily along, Tony had Benny Peluso, the former Bruno lieutenant, who had been captured and forced to talk, brought before him. After all, the success of his present campaign was due largely to the information which Benny had unwillingly given.

The squat, ugly gangster looked sullen and more than a little frightened as he came in between the two gunmen who originally had captured him and brought him in.

"Well, Benny," said Tony, "the dope you gave me has proved O.K. And here's the dough I promised you," tossing *an* envelope across the desk. "These men will take you to a train bound for the West; they're to guard you from any of the Bruno mob who may try to get you."

The little gangster who had been compelled to squeal on his associates for a price seized the envelope and greedily thumbed through the fifteen $1,000 bills it contained. Then he looked up at Tony and smiled gratefully. In gangland, it was indeed a pleasure to find an enemy—or even a friend—who kept his word when he didn't have to.

"T'anks," he said. "I didn't t'ink you'd come t'rough!"

"I always keep my word—good or bad," retorted Tony, his former enemy's sincere gratitude touching him as much as anything could. "On your way—and good luck!"

Tony's own gunmen, the dapper, polished Mike Rinaldo in command of the little party, escorted Peluso away. An hour later, Rinaldo returned, looking rather downcast.

"Got a little bad news to report, chief,"- he said. "On the way down to the depot, another car forced us into the curb and a coupla hoods bumped Benny off before we could pull our gats. We jumped out of the car and beat it before the cops came. Some of the Bruno mob must have found out we had him here and been on the lookout for him to come out."

"All right," said Tony wearily. "I s'pose the cops and newspapers will blame me for having him bumped off because so far as they know he was still an enemy of ours.... See that we get the car back."

Tony thought over that report for some time after the dapper but dangerous Rinaldo had gone. He was wise in the ways of gunmen and he had a strong hunch that Rinaldo and his assistant had murdered Peluso themselves for the $15,000. But there would be no way of pinning it on them; the savage enmity that the Bruno mob was sure to feel against Peluso if they suspected what he had done prevented direct suspicion being leveled against the two gunmen. Well, what was the difference; he had kept his end of the deal in good faith, and Peluso was a yellow rat anyway. In his heart, Tony knew that they were all yellow rats when faced with a situation that demanded character and moral courage. His suspicions were verified, to a certain extent, when Rinaldo appeared the following week driving an expensive new car.

Tony again directed his attention to the campaign against the North Side outfit with undiminished zest. For Schemer Bruno was not lying supine under the onslaught of his enemies. He was fighting back with every resource of his wily, daring brain and his strong organization. Altogether it was as desperate a reign of terror as has ever been produced on this continent in time of peace. And the newspapers began to howl about the rights of citizens, the danger to the lives and property of innocent bystanders.

"Damn 'em!" growled Tony to Jane one night. "Don't they know that we don't hurt nobody but hoods? Neither me nor any of my men ever hit anybody except the mugg we was after. And I never heard of any other mob that did. And we never throw a pineapple unless we know what's goin' on inside the place. If decent citizens own some of the property, let 'em keep the racketeers out; you can't tell me that a man don't know what's goin' on in a building he owns. If he wants to take the chance to get a bigger rent, he's no better than the hoodlums he rents to and he's got to take the chance of the place being blown up."

But the next morning Tony received a telephone call from the District Attorney.

"Camonte?" demanded the familiar overbearing voice. "I want to see you this afternoon. Suite F, in the Sherman Hotel. Two o'clock sharp."

"Why not at the office?" objected Tony. "What's up, anyhow?"

"Never mind. Be there, that's all." And the D.A. hung up.

Until one-thirty Tony puzzled over that official command. He couldn't figure it out. For a while he suspected a trap and almost decided not to go, then he realized that the District Attorney would not dare to be in on a murder plot against a leader as prominent as he. But one thing certain, it boded no good.

He was still sunk in gloomy and somewhat uneasy thought when he rode downtown accompanied by his bodyguard. Piling out of their two cars in front of the huge hotel, the men formed a close circle around him and escorted him inside. They crowded quickly into an empty elevator, practically filling it, then commanded the operator to take them to Suite F, and "make it snappy." The operator hesitated, waiting for two or three more passengers, then took another look at those he already had and obeyed their command.

Released into the hallway of an upper floor, the entire party was immediately surrounded and taken in hand by a dozen detectives, who began disarming them with systematic and none too gentle thoroughness.

"Hey! What's the idea anyhow?" demanded Tony belligerently.

"You'll find out soon enough," retorted a burly dick. "Pass over your gats, too. There's goin' to be nobody bumped off here today."

Tony ground his teeth but he offered no resistance. Killing a detective in the heat and obscurity of an alley gun battle was one thing while shooting one deliberately in a prominent hotel in the presence of a dozen of his fellows was quite another. But Tony was outwardly very indignant and inwardly very uneasy. His followers were silent and docile,, as modern gangsters always are when disarmed and outnumbered.

When the disarmament program had been completed, the crowd was led down the hall to an open doorway and Tony's henchmen were herded inside.

"You're to stay in here until we come after you," said the detective who seemed to be in command. "And don't make any fuss or we'll take you down to the bureau and give you all a treatment with the rubber hoses we keep on hand for hoodlums like you."

Then he locked the door, pocketed the key, and leaving two of his men on guard before the portal, led Tony on down the hall to a closed door marked *F.* He knocked, then opened the door and practically shoved Tony inside. Tony heard the door shut behind him and a key grate in the lock. Then his glance riveted upon the scene of which he had become a part and he stiffened.

Around a large table in the middle of the luxurious parlor sat half a dozen men. There was one empty chair, evidently for him. Tony recognized all those men. At the head of the table, alone, sat the District Attorney, a squat, slightly corpulent man with mean little eyes and a heavy, bulldog jaw. The other men included every prominent gang leader in the city and county, including Schemer Bruno.

"Come on and sit down, Camonte," snapped the D.A. brusquely. "The meeting's ready to begin."

Tony walked forward slowly, assuming a bold air of cool calm that he did not feel, and sat down, glaring at Bruno, who allowed a slight smile to curve the lips of his lean, handsome face as he noted Tony's left arm in its sling. It was their first meeting.

"What's the matter with your arm?" he asked. His tone and manner were polite, yet there was an underlying note of contempt and amusement that made Tony's blood boil.

"I was in an auto wreck the other night," retorted Tony. "But there were other people hurt, too," he added with grim relish as he remembered that overturned car with its cargo of dead and injured.

Bruno's smile faded like a dab of dirt that is wiped away with a quick dash of a cloth and his face froze into a hard, expressionless mask in which the eyes were the only sign of life. But they burned with an intense, malevolent hatred. From his own feelings, Tony knew that Bruno's right hand was itching for a gun.

"That'll do," snapped the D.A. "I'm doing the talking today."

The six men, most important of the city's underworld leaders and representing its every element except petty thievery, turned and looked at the man who was the most powerful of the law-enforcing agencies, the man who had been elected by trusting citizens to protect them from the machinations and henchmen of the men with whom he now sat in conference. All were paying him heavily and all despised him, feeling for him the contempt that must always be the lot of the one who betrays his trust. Yet secretly they all feared the great power which was his, the extermination which he could mete out to them if he wished.

"This war's got to stop!" exclaimed the D.A., pounding the desk to emphasize his command. "The newspapers are raising hell and even some of the big politicians are worried about it. Some of the influential men here have gone to the governor and told him that the city's getting such a bad name people are afraid to come here and that it's hurting business. There's even talk of appointing a special prosecutor—some wealthy, fearless lawyer who couldn't be reached—and a special grand jury to investigate the gang situation. And you know what that would mean."

The gang leaders shifted uneasily. They did know what such an investigation would mean—a lot of unpleasantness and, perhaps, extinction.

"Camonte," continued the D.A., glaring at Tony, "I know that you and Bruno are the guilty ones in this latest outbreak, the most savage we've ever experienced. But I also know that the only reason you other fellows aren't in it is because you're not big enough to compete with these two and you've got sense enough to know it... There's enough business here for all of you and you've got to declare a truce and operate peaceably, all taking your share."

"Do you think *he'd* keep a truce?" demanded Bruno, with a contemptuous nod at Tony.

"You wouldn't, that's one damn sure thing," blazed Tony, his mouth curled into a nasty snarl.

"I wouldn't dare to—with you. Who wants to be shot in the back?"

"Why, you dirty—"

"Shut up!" snapped the D.A. savagely. "And listen to me. Or I'll run you out of town."

"You'd lose a good part of your income if you did," sneered Tony, roused to fury by his altercation with Bruno.

Stung to anger by the impudent remark, the D.A. frowned and turned upon him a baleful glare.

"I'd better have a part of my income than none at all," he retorted through gritted teeth. "Another crack like that out of you and *you'll* be the first to go."

Tony subsided but he was seething with fury. Given sufficient time he would get all his enemies, perhaps even the D.A. himself. Stranger things had happened, and he certainly had it coming to him.

The District Attorney had spread out on the table a large map of the county, which included the large city which took up most of it. Already the map was divided by red lines and inside of each square thus produced was written the name of one of the men present.

"Here are the territories I've assigned to each of you," continued the D.A. "And I think all of you will agree that I have been very fair. You big fellows have been allotted most of it, of course, but the little mobs have their proportionate share because they have to get along, too."

The gang leaders stared at the map. And in their own hearts they all realized that the D.A. had made a fair division of the territory. Each of them also realized that within the district assigned to him for sovereignty lay sufficient business to keep him and his mob busy and to make them exceedingly prosperous. Yet their code had always been to hold their own territory and fight the other fellow for his, just as they expected him to fight them for theirs. And to the victor belonged the spoils of both.

"Here are other maps just like this one, a copy for each of you, with your territories outlined on it," continued the D.A., passing the folded papers around. "And the first man who oversteps his bounds gets run out of town, I don't care who he is. Furthermore, you are to report this arrangement to your respective gangs, acquainting them thoroughly with the limits in which they may operate, and see that they obey. Each man is responsible for the acts of his mob; if he can't control his men and make them obey his orders, he's not fit to be leading the mob. *And no more shooting, or I'm going to prosecute the guilty people for murder, I don't care who they are....* You can go now—Camonte, you first with your men. You others can go later one by one after he and his bodyguard have left. And be sure you leave at once, Camonte. I have detectives watching outside and any loitering in the expectation of exacting vengeance upon anybody here will be met with arrests and prosecution."

Tony rose and surveyed the gathering, giving Bruno a particularly thorough stare, then turned and strode out of the room. For him, the conference had served one good purpose—he had met Schemer Bruno face to face.

He knew exactly what his arch enemy looked like and, from now on, would be able to identify him with certainty even at some little distance. Which was a great help for accurate night shooting.

chapter 19

For a while, almost four months in fact, things were quiet. Everybody was making money and there were no killings. Then the men began to grow restive, as men of action will after a certain period of inactivity. The resumption of hostilities began with minor affrays between insignificant members of the various gangs which usually resulted in nothing more serious than bloody noses and black eyes. Then an occasional stabbing began to creep in among the hitherto comparatively harmless sport, and finally a shooting or two. The anxiety for action, for war and vengeance, became more marked. A tense air of watchful waiting, of incipient menace, hung over the headquarters of the various gangs. The men mentally were like bloodhounds straining at the leash.

Tony sensed the situation. He was weary of inactivity himself. And he was becoming suspicious of the prolonged quietude of his enemies. He knew that they and their men were no more capable of interminable peace than were he and his mob. It was rapidly narrowing to a question of who would strike first.

Among Tony's various valuable possessions were a number of gambling places. One of these was a second-floor establishment in the heart of the city. Despite its central position, it was located on a street which contained no department stores and in a block which consisted of wholesale barber supply stores and other such enterprises which dealt with few customers. Which made foot traffic on its sidewalks quite light.

Tony visited the place almost every day, a fact which he had never tried to conceal. As he stepped out of his sedan in front of the place one afternoon and paused an instant for his bodyguard to gather around him, he heard the sudden stuttering rat-tat-tat of a machine gun. He saw two of his bodyguard go down before the deadly hail of lead and the others, darting low to take advantage of all the shelter the two sedans offered, look frantically about in an effort to find the source of the attack. Tony himself leaped inside the doorway that led to his second-floor establishment, but not before he felt a dozen heavy blows against his body. The marksmanship of his assailants had been deadly accurate, all right, but he was wearing a bullet-proof vest.

In the comparative shelter of the narrow hall that led to the stairway, he turned. Already his automatic was out, ready for execution. He could see two of his men firing upward at the windows of the small hotel across the street. But with his own disappearance the vicious stuttering of the machine gun had ceased. He imagined that the attackers already were in flight, trying desperately to make their escape before the arrival of the police. And his own men must do the same, to avoid arrest and serious charges. A daylight gun battle in a downtown street was no simple matter to adjust with the authorities.

He stepped to the doorway and searched the windows of the hotel with a quick but careful glance. He saw nothing suspicious.

"Cut it!" he snapped. "Into the cars, quick! Let's go!"

He made a flying leap for one of the sedans and clambered in. The men piled in around him and into ' the other machine. The two big cars roared away down the street. With only inches to spare, they swerved around a traffic cop who was frantically blowing his whistle at them, and raced onward, bound for home and safety. Tony's eyes were glittering with cold, deadly fury but within him he felt a great exultation. The war was on again!

"They was on the third floor of the hotel, boss," panted one of the men. "We seen 'em plain—two of 'em. One of 'em was usin' a Thompson and the other one had a automatic."

A Thompson is that particular type of machine gun which is the favorite weapon of the modern gangster, an easily transported but wicked death machine which can be handled with the ease of a rifle and which, while weighing only ten pounds, will hurl one hundred bullets per minutes.

When they reached headquarters, Tony went immediately to his private office and telephoned the District Attorney.

"They just tried to get me from the third floor of the Victor Hotel," he said almost gleefully.

"I know. I just got a flash on it from the detective bureau."

"Must have been some of the Bruno mob. What are you going to do about it?"

"Just what I promised at that last conference. As many of the North Side mob as we can get our hands on will he rounded up tonight, questioned and brought into court in the morning."

Which sounded fine, thought Tony, but didn't mean a thing. The chances were very strong that the actual assailants had made a clean getaway, none of the others would talk—in fact, they would probably know nothing of the attack until they saw it in the papers or were arrested—and the D.A.'s office would be able to prove against them nothing more serious than a charge of carrying concealed weapons. Tony realized that the whole round-up and subsequent activity would really amount to nothing more than a grand gesture for the benefit of the newspapers to pass on to the public.

But, Tony felt that a round-up like that was too great an opportunity to be lost. He called in a dozen of his most reliable gunmen and for an hour drilled them in the details of a plan which would be the most daring gangland gesture the city had yet seen.

The evening papers—always more sensational than those published in the morning—made a great fuss over the afternoon attack, giving it huge headlines and a great deal of space. And some of the information was of the afternoon attack, giving it huge headlines and a great deal of space. And some of the information was of great interest to Tony. The police, in the search of the hotel following the attack, had found in a third-floor room fronting the street a Thompson machine gun, an empty automatic and a dead man with half a dozen bullets in him. *And the dead man later had been identified as Stave Libati.*

"The dirty—!" breathed Tony venomously. "Turned traitor, did he? And some of the boys got him. Either that or his own partner shot him in the back, afraid that he might turn him up later. Well, anyway, he sure had it coming to him."

Tony studied over the various angles of the occurrence for some time. The identification of one of the assailants as his former lieutenant brought in a new element. There was a chance, of course, that Steve had carried out the attack as a matter of personal vengeance. But it wasn't likely. He didn't have that much brains. No, the affair had been planned out by the crafty Schemer Bruno, who had used the ready Libati as a cat's paw. The chances were that Steve, upon being fired by Tony, had joined the North Side outfit, being admitted because of the valuable information he could furnish Bruno and because of his avowed hatred of Tony.

The morning papers, while showing a trifle more reserve about the whole matter, carried the news that the most thorough dragnet of years had been sent through the North Side during the night, with the result that a large portion of the notorious North Side gang—including the wily Schemer himself—had been rounded up and were now reposing in cells, from which they would be removed for court appearances that morning on various charges.

At nine-thirty, Tony loaded his dozen carefully selected gunmen into two big sedans and set forth on the little expedition he had planned the day before. When slightly less than a block away from the police court where Tony knew the North Side mob would be arraigned, he ordered the cars parked—but with their engines kept running for an instant getaway—and instructed his men to spread out along the street. He watched them take their stations then smiled coldly with pleased anticipation. When Schemer Bruno and his men came out—as they were sure to do—they would get a terrific surprise. And of course, just coming from court, they would be unarmed. It looked as though this morning would put a terrible dent in the North Side mob.

Suddenly the double doors of the police station—the court was above a station—swung open and a stream of detectives and uniformed officers streamed out and bore down on Tony's men.

"Hell!" gritted Tony, who had remained sitting beside the chauffeur in one of the cars. "The cops have seen 'em. Step on it!"

The big car roared into life and swerved around the corner, but not before two shots had rung out in the street and two bullets had thudded against the rear of the machine.

"Stop!" commanded Tony, and the car ground to a halt. Close as they were to the station, they were out of sight of it. "Gimme your gat!"

The chauffeur quickly handed over his revolver and Tony calmly dropped it down a convenient open sewer. He tossed his own heavy automatic after it then removed his small vest-pocket automatic from its customary position and shoved it down inside of one sock. When two detectives came puffing around the corner with ready revolvers—as he knew they would—he was standing calmly beside the car.

"Did you want to talk to me?" he demanded with a frown.

"I'll say so," panted one. "It's lucky Lieutenant Grady looked out the window and recognized some of them gorillas of yours hangin' around outside, or we'd a had a whole streetful o' murders on our hands."

"Lieutenant Grady, was it?" queried Tony pleasantly. "I'll have to remember that."

"I don't care what you remember. Just come along quietly, both o' you muggs."

"Got a warrant?"

"Naw, 'course not."

"What's the charge?"

"Carryin' concealed weapons."

"But I'm not carrying concealed weapons."

"Naw?" exclaimed the burly detective incredulously. "Humph! Tryin' to stall, eh? Keep the rod on 'em, Jim, while I frisk 'em."

Quickly and thoroughly he searched Tony, but of course he did not extend it below the knees. Obviously puzzled, he hauled the chauffeur out of the car and searched him—without result. With evident bewilderment he surveyed these two men on whom he knew he should find guns. Then an idea occurred to him, as it sometimes does to an unusually bright police detective.

"I got it!" he exclaimed with sudden enthusiasm. "You dropped 'em on the floor or hid 'em in the car some place. That's an old trick of birds like you."

He went at the car as if he were going to take it apart. And he did as well as he could without the aid of dynamite or tools. But he found nothing incriminating.

"You see?" said Tony. "I told you the truth. I'm just out for a little drive this morning. And I don't like being shot at without reason when motoring." He produced two $50 bills and passed one to each of the puzzled detectives. "Now, boys, buy yourselves some cigars and forget that you ever saw me in this neighborhood this morning. And I won't tell anybody what a silly trick you pulled."

He climbed into his car and drove away, within three blocks removing the small automatic from his sock and placing it in his coat pocket ready for an emergency.

"Jeez! Boss, that was smooth work!" exclaimed the chauffeur admiringly.

"If the cops was as sharp as we are, we wouldn't have a chance!" answered Tony wisely.

From his private office at his headquarters, he telephoned Captain Flanagan.

"This is Tony Camonte!" he said brusquely. "I hear they picked up some of my men out at Lawrence Avenue."

"Yeah. Just heard about it."

"Well, how about springin' 'em? I ought to get some service for that monthly bit."

"Sorry, Tony, but there isn't a hell of a lot I can do. If they was here at the bureau, it would be different, but it would look funny if I interfered too much out there. Some snoopy reporter might find out about it and shoot the works. I'll see, though, that none of 'em are booked for anything more than concealed weapons. But you better send down a mouthpiece to front for 'em."

So Tony telephoned one of the able attorneys on his staff to go out and represent his men at their hearing, then fell into a mood of vengeful brooding. One plan had failed. *The next one must not.*

chapter 20

In his mail one morning Tony Camonte received a unique communication, an ornate, engraved invitation to the opening of the Woodland Casino, a new road-house and gambling place some little distance out in the country, far beyond the jurisdiction of city authorities but not so far away as to be beyond the reach of city patrons. The invitation also conveyed the information that the opening night was to be a Bal Masque and that admittance would be by card only.

Tony didn't know what a Bal Masque was and he felt no urge to find out. But the other bit of information interested him somewhat. In common with other wealthy but socially ineligible people, he had an almost irresistible curiosity to see the inside of exclusive places. The realization that hundreds of these invitations must have been sent out did not prevent his own vanity being tickled by receiving one; the fact remained that *everybody* who might want to couldn't get in.

For a moment he toyed with the pleasant thought that he was getting to be a man of some importance in the city. Then his suspicion of everything and everybody, born of native cunning and bitter experience, asserted itself. The thing was probably a plant of some kind; perhaps an attempt to put him on a spot. He looked closely at the enclosed engraved card. There seemed to be no identifying marks upon it but his momentary illusion of possible social grandeur had been dispelled by his innate caution. Half the gangsters in town were sure to be at a place like that; it sounded like just the sort of layout that appealed to them for sport. But did they think he'd be simple enough to fall for a game like that?

He crumpled the invitation and card with strong, tense fingers and tossed them in the wastebasket.

A few minutes later the telephone at his elbow rang. It was Jane.

"Could you run home a few minutes, dear?" she asked. "I have something very important to tell you."

"Tell me now."

"Can't. You never can tell when some nosy mugg—a cop or somebody—is listening in on a phone."

"Won't it wait till tonight?"

"Yes, I s'pose so," doubtfully. "But I wish you'd come now."

"Oh, all right," growled Tony.

So he summoned his bodyguard and went home, ordering them to remain outside while he hurried up to his luxurious apartment, a vague uneasiness clutching at him. But Jane was happy and smiling.

"Darling!" she exclaimed happily. "I've found the spot where we can get Bruno.... He's going to the opening of the new Woodland Casino tomorrow night. That's our chance."

Tony's sharp gaze narrowed.

"Yeah?" he said. "How'd you find that out?"

"Don't ask me, please. I'm not very proud of the way I got the dope but *I did* get it—that's all that matters. And that's our big chance to bump him off, Tony. He won't be looking for trouble at an affair like that and he won't have a big bodyguard with him— maybe none at all. Anyway it's a masked affair—everybody will be in costume and wearing masks—so nobody'll know who we are."

"No? Then how'll we know who *they* are?"

"It's up to us to find out."

"Well, I'll think about it."

He returned to his headquarters and, rescuing the all-important admission card from the wastebasket, thought about it for the rest of the afternoon. Something warned him not to go, yet the chance of killing Bruno himself proved a temptation too strong to resist. He decided to assume the risk.

The next morning, accompanied by four of his bodyguard, he went down and looked at costumes. But he selected nothing, because he did not want the costumer to know his disguise. He was afraid that such information might be passed on to his enemies and he realized fully that his safety lay in the strict preservation of his anonymity. But in the afternoon he sent down another man for a Henry the Eighth outfit. In his mind, he had chosen that during the morning inspection because a comfortable amount of artillery could be concealed under the voluminous velvet upper part and the false beard that went with it would effectually hide the scar on the left side of his face.

He and Jane—she was lovely in a Juliet costume— drove out shortly after ten, taking with them a bodyguard of four fearless and expert gunmen. Two of the latter, who were sufficiently small and slender to get away with it were in feminine costumes, so that it seemed like a nice party of three couples. Tony had had one of his men rent a sedan for the night, a much smaller and less expensive car than he ever used, so that neither car nor license could give them away to possible watchful enemies. Yet it was a very fast car—he had made sure of that.

A hundred yards from the place, Tony halted the car and they all affixed their masks. Then he drove up and parked facing the road. Tony was a little uneasy about the admittance of so large a party on the one card but the doorman, masked and attired in the ornate costume of a Turkish harem guard, bowed them all inside with eager welcome. With how eager a welcome, Tony had no idea. For there were certain things about this affair that Jane had not discovered and that he had not suspected. *For instance, Jane had not found out that Schemer Bruno was the owner of this new place and Tony had never dreamed that the card sent to him was the only one which bore the word "Gambling" engraved in the lower left-hand corner.* Thus they were identified the moment they entered the place. In fact, they were the guests of honor but they didn't know it.

The Woodland Casino was unusually spacious and elaborate for a place of its type. A large dining room, arranged in cabaret style with a dance floor in the center, occupied most of the first floor. A good orchestra blared toe-tickling jazz from a dais at one end and waiters scurried about with trays of food and drinks. Tony and his party, unknowingly under the murderous gaze of a dozen pairs of eyes, casually surveyed the throng present, then moved upstairs.

The second floor was divided into numerous gaming rooms, in which could be found every imaginable device for pitting one's luck against the game-keeper's skill. All the play was for high stakes. Tony abstractedly took a whirl at roulette and because he wasn't interested in the game, caring for neither profits nor losses, won more than two thousand dollars in half an hour. The *croupier,* hoping to win it back for the house, urged him to continue but Tony shook his head and led his party away from the table.

They went back downstairs. The crowd was bigger now and very gay. The noise was fearful yet somehow diverting. Tony and his accomplices would have enjoyed it a lot except for their deadly errand. Tony himself was tense and silent, as he always was just before pulling a job of murder. In whispers, he instructed his henchmen not to stick so closely to him as to excite suspicion, but to maintain a keen watch. He danced three or four time's with Jane, his gunmen dancing close by. Then he led her aside.

"Mix around a little," he ordered. "See if you can find out whether Bruno's here and if he is, what kind of a rig he's got on."

Jane nodded and moved slowly away. Tony allowed his penetrating glance to make a deliberate search of the merry throng. If only he knew how Bruno was dressed. Here and there, he noted subconsciously an exceptionally striking woman. Then abruptly his gaze riveted to the most commanding feminine figure in the crowd. Tall and slender she was, regally attired in an obviously expensive white gown with a long court train. Resting atop her head to complete the effect was an ornate crown studded with flashing brilliants.

She was walking when he saw her first and it was her walk that struck him particularly. It was graceful, regal, the proper walk for the Queen she represented. And he had seen it before somewhere. He tried to recall and found he couldn't. But he was certain he had seen that identical walk before and, subconsciously, he knew that the remembrance was not pleasant.

He watched her closely, still trying to remember, and found her receiving a great deal of attention from a cloaked figure of Satan, a tall, well-built, graceful man who moved with the lithe quickness of a trained body actuated by an agile mind.

At last she moved away from her red-clad companion and began drifting toward him. She hesitated as she came opposite and looked at him deliberately. The mask made the glance curiously enigmatic yet the sparkling eyes behind the mask seemed to hold an invitation. Then she moved away again. Reaching the doorway, she paused and looked back, then stepped through the portal. It was all as plain as if she had spoken. She was going out on the big wide porch and inviting him to follow. Momentarily warming to the chase, he started forward impulsively.

But at that instant he suddenly remembered where he had seen that walk before. She was Katherine Merton, the girl who had come to his office pretending to be a reporter and who, in reality, was Schemer Bruno's moll. Then Satan must be Bruno. What a singularly appropriate costume for the Schemer, he thought. And that cloak would conceal an almost unlimited amount of artillery. He saw the whole plot in a flash now. How they had discovered his identity, he couldn't imagine—but they *had*. And this moll was trying to lure him out on the porch so that they could bump him off without endangering the other customers. Clever, all right, but it wasn't going to work.

He darted upstairs and cautiously peered out a window. Four or five costumed and masked figures were moving slowly around in front of the place. *And the cloaked devil was among them.* It was a death plot all right.

He hurried back downstairs and without any appearance of haste gathered his group around him.

"Take Jane out and put her in the car," he ordered one of the gunmen, one also dressed as a woman. "Don't hurry,... but have the car ready for a quick getaway.... The rest of you come with me."

He knew that Jane and her companion would not be targets for assassins' bullets. It was he they were after. He led his three gunmen toward the kitchen, to the right of which was a mahogany bar, now three deep with thirsty patrons. There would surely be another entrance from the kitchen. Then he saw it, an open doorway. Before the surprised chef and his assistants could object, Tony had led his gunmen across the kitchen and out into the night. Quickly but silently they stole forward and Tony cautiously peered around the corner of the building. The waiting men were still there, tensely expectant. On the porch, a white-clad figure was glancing back into the reception foyer. Evidently the moll couldn't understand why he didn't appear.

"See those muggs out there?" demanded Tony in a hoarse whisper. "That's Schemer Bruno and some of his mob waitin' to get us. But we're goin' to beat 'em to it. You guys take care of the rest of 'em. I'll get the devil."

Slowly Tony lifted his heavy automatic and took careful aim. Then his steady trigger finger squeezed down and the weapon spoke with a thunderous flash. Elation surged through him as the red-clad figure staggered and crumpled to the ground, but he fired four more times with deliberate precision at the prone figure. His men were firing, too. Revolvers were flashing and cracking ill around him. But the others were fighting back. At the first shot they had all dropped to the ground, making themselves much smaller targets, and now they were firing savagely. Tony and his men could hear bullets whistling and thudding around them. At first there were four exploding revolvers in that line, then three... two... one. And finally it ceased.

"Let's go!" exclaimed Tony happily and ran for their car, fifteen yards away.

They all piled in and it raced away at high speed.

"Step on it!" commanded Tony. He knew there were more enemy gunmen inside that roadhouse and he didn't care to battle them if it could be avoided. He looked back just in time to see a white-clad figure crumple to the floor of the porch and other people come streaming out through the double door.

"God! that was a narrow squeak!" exclaimed Tony as the car raced back toward their headquarters. "If I hadn't remembered that dame's walk, they'd a got me sure as hell. They damn near put over a fast one! Say," he said suddenly, turning on Jane with angry suspicion, "what do you know about this, anyhow?"

"Why, what do you mean?"

"You know damn well what I mean," he growled. "Didn't you know they had it all fixed to put me on a spot?"

"Of course not! Tony, surely—"

"Well, where'd you get the dope about him bein' out here tonight?"

"From Katherine—his moll."

"From *who?* For God's sake, how'd you get her to talk?'

"She's—my sister."

"Oh, my God! Here I've been a sort of brother-in-law to the Schemer, my worst enemy, all this time. Jeez! What a fine family mess I got into."

"I thought I was pumping her when we met yesterday, making her tell something that she didn't want to," continued Jane in a strained voice. She was overwrought and on the verge of tears. "But I guess I only fell into the trap she was helping the Schemer bait for you."

"Well, it's all right," answered Tony generously. "We got the Schemer anyhow."

Schemer Bruno's sudden and mysterious death was a city-wide sensation for days. His funeral was a grand affair, attended by the District Attorney, the Chief of Police, eleven judges, and some two hundred carloads of politicians and other hoodlums. Tony sent a $200 floral piece and considered it the best investment he had ever made. His only regret about the affair was that he hadn't had cause to send it sooner.

chapter 21

A year passed rather uneventfully. Tony's power, undisputed save for sporadic, disorganized, short-lived outbreaks here and there, grew until it almost became burdensome. And his income had gone far beyond his wildest dreams. Always being written up and talked about but almost never seen, he had become a legendary figure, symbolical of underworld success.

Two items in the papers concerning his own family had interested him. His father had died and his brother had been promoted to a detective lieutenancy. Tony's answer to the first had been to arrange for one of his trusted attorneys to inform his mother of the death of some mysterious relative in the West and thereafter pay her $1,000 a month, supposedly from the deceased's estate. His answer to the second had been a long, loud, ironical laugh. He had heard through various reliable sources that his brother was not averse to graft and was quite a devil with the women, despite his wife and child. Tony grinned when he thought what a stir there would be if it were discovered that the brother of Detective Lieutenant Ben Guarino was the famous gang leader, Scarface Tony Camonte.

He and Jane were still together, constantly quarreling a bit more, but still together. They moved often, as often as the owners of the luxurious apartment houses to which they confined their residence discovered their real identities. But they enjoyed the best of everything and waved wads of money in the envious faces of the stiff-backed "genteels" who snubbed them. Tony had no fault to find with the world so far. Success wasn't difficult, if you weren't squeamish about how you achieved it. He surmised wisely that many another millionaire had discovered that fact early in his career.

But inactivity palled on Tony! He stretched and began looking around for new worlds to conquer. People said the East—New York—was the most lucrative liquor and racket section in the country. There were a lot of hoodlums in it, of course, but they weren't used to the ruthless Middle West methods. Machine guns and bombs would give the more effete Easterners the surprise of their lives.

At about that same time rumors that the Easterners were looking westward with avaricious eyes gained circulation and credence. It was said that the notorious Frankie Wales, most ruthless of the Eastern gang leaders, was planning an active campaign for the Middle West with the Middle West's own methods and weapons. But Tony only laughed contemptuously when his lieutenants came to him with such stories. He was too powerful, too well known even in New York for any other leader to even dream of wresting his power and wealth away from him. But the suggestion of another hot battle brought back the old sparkle to his eyes. If anybody tried to cut in on him, he'd show them a thing or two. He'd not only hold his territory but he'd capture theirs, wherever it might be and whoever it might be.

Tony didn't believe the reports of the Eastern invasion until one night when he was eating dinner in the main floor dining room of his hotel headquarters. The sudden crash of shattering glass and the vicious stuttering of a machine gun in the street outside startled him from his complacent reverie. He ducked under the table and drew his automatic. That nasty rat-tat-tat was still going in the street, the big plate glass window up in front was still splintering. And he could hear whizzing bullets whining spitefully above his head. Then the machine guns hushed and he heard a powerful car roar away. There was no doubt as to whom they were after. Had he been a second later in dodging beneath the table, his well-tailored form would have been drilled by a score of bullets; the holes in the wall back of where he had been sitting proved that.

He remembered suddenly that the North Side mob had scared Johnny Lovo into leaving town by that same trick. Well, whoever had pulled it this time, would find he wasn't afraid of anything. If they wanted a war, they could have one. And he'd be glad to see that they got a good one.

That his unknown enemies meant business was proved by their activities the rest of the night. They bombed his biggest warehouse and killed two of his henchmen who were driving the sedan which he ordinarily used. Things were picking up. Tony smiled with keen anticipation.

Walking quickly into the lobby of the hotel the next night, following a tour of inspection and preparation at various outposts of his activities, Tony saw two people getting into the elevator. Mike Rinaldo, his prize gunman, and a girl. But the glimpse he got of the girl's face . before the door clanged shut and the car shot upward made his eyes widen and his breath catch. Surely it must be—

He turned to a small group of his henchmen lounging near by.

"That girl who just went up with Mike," he said slowly, coldly. "Do any of you know who she is?"

"Why that's one of the sweetest little propositions that's turned up around here in a long time. But particular—Jeez! Mike's the only guy in the mob that's been able to make her so far. Her name is—lemmesee—I think it's Rosie Guarino."

"God!" breathed Tony hoarsely.

"What's the matter, chief?"

"N-Nothing," answered Tony breathlessly. But his face had gone deathly white.

His thoughts seemed to be trying to race frantically up a terribly steep hill. Rosie, his little sister Rosie, the one that had always been such a model little housekeeper while their mother tended to the store. He realized suddenly that she must be twenty-two or three now. And he had been thinking of her as a beautiful kid of sixteen. But here in this disreputable hotel, gone upstairs with Mike Rinaldo, the accomplished and unscrupulous heart-breaker who was the best gunman in the city... His sister.... No, it mustn't be.... If she hadn't sense enough herself, somebody else—

He walked over to the desk, his step a trifle unsteady, his eyes glazed in contemplation of a horror more terrible than any he had seen on French battlefields.

"What number did you give Mike Rinaldo?" he asked.

"Six-twelve," answered the clerk. "But a lady went up with him, Mr. Camonte. Wouldn't it be better to calf?"

"Thanks. I—I'll call him later."

He walked over and entered the elevator, which had come back down.

"Six," he said dully and swayed a little from the sudden jerk as the car started upward.

He had killed for money, for vengeance, for lust, for almost every reason except a worthy one. His sister... Upstairs... In his own hotel... With one of his own gunmen... Of course, Mike was the straightest and most ruthless shot in the city. Tony realized he might be facing death, probably was. Mike was touchy about his heart affairs. But Tony had faced death before. He'd always won before. One of these days he was bound to lose—luck couldn't run the same way all the time. But whichever way things went, he would always be facing it.

The door clanged open and Tony stepped out into the hall, his right hand plunged deep into his side coat pocket, his lean fingers tensed about the cold butt of the heavy automatic there.

chapter 22

Slowly, yet with a tense, frantic haste, Scarface Tony Camonte went down the hall; peering intently at the brass numbers on the doors, his hand rigid about the butt of the heavy automatic in his side coat pocket.

Then he found it. 612. He halted and turned toward the door, gathering himself like a furious animal making ready to spring. With the silent, effortless ease of a fatal snake, his practiced right hand drew the automatic, then gently dropped to his side. Then his left hand reached out to the door-knob, and he quietly tried it. But the door was locked.

Tony's lips curled into a vicious snarl and his clenched fist banged savagely against the polished wood of the fastened door. There was a pause. Then:

"What do you want?" came the angry growl from within.

"Come out here!" snapped Tony, and instinctively moved aside so that when the door opened he would not be visible.

"Go 'way and lemme alone," came the retort. "I'm busy."

The gang leader's face flamed with rage and his breath came in short, hoarse gasps.

"This is Tony Camonte, the boss," he gritted, his mouth close to the crack where the door met the jamb. "I want to see you now. If you don't come out, I'll send for a pass-key and come in."

He drew back again and his grip on the automatic tightened. He heard muffled sounds of stirring within the room and a feminine giggle. And he muttered an awful curse under his breath as the key turned in the lock. The door swung open.

"Say, chief, what the hell's the matter with you, anyway?" demanded Mike Rinaldo's voice.

Then Mike himself appeared. His coat and vest were off, his collar open at the throat. His handsome dark face was flushed and his oily black hair tousled. His appearance alone was enough, under the circumstances, to give Tony the final impulse to murder, to furnish the igniting spark for the ready powder. Surprised and angry, Mike turned to face his employer.

Tony's right hand snapped up and the ugly black barrel of the automatic centered steadily on the gunman's body a few inches above his shining gold belt buckle.

"You rat!" snarled Tony. "You picked the wrong dame this time."

The two pairs of cold, hard, expressionless eyes, murderers' eyes both, met, clashed. Then Mike's widened at something he saw in those of his employer. He was staring death in the face and he realized it. His right hand darted for his hip. But he hadn't a chance; Tony didn't dare give him a chance. Under any other conditions, Tony would have been glad to meet him on even terms, but now the great gang leader felt that he dare not take any risks. He must make sure, because of that girl in there.

In the language of their kind, Tony let him have it. The shots roared out. Half a dozen of them. Yet so close together that they seemed to merge into a single explosion as they reverberated down the hall. Mike's jaw dropped and he gazed stupidly at his murderer through the haze of a bluish smoke. Then he passed a trembling hand bewilderedly over his suddenly ashen face and with a gasp abruptly sagged to the floor. Half a dozen spots of red had appeared on his hitherto spotless white shirt-front. Tony watched with interest as they enlarged, then finally merged into one big stain that grew bigger.

Suddenly Tony laughed, a little hysterically. Then he became aware that the girl inside the room was screaming madly. That screaming cleared his head like a dash of cold water. With his foot, he moved the body beyond the doorway, then walked into the room. A beautiful dark girl, clad in pink silk lingerie and with a dress clutched in her hands, stood there shrieking.

Her eyes dilated with terror as she saw him come in and she backed away, lifting one hand as if to ward off an attack. Tony stared at her a moment, feeling the bitter agony of coals of fire being heaped upon his head. His sister! To be found like that! But he was thankful that she didn't recognize him.

"Shut up!" he snapped. "Get your dress on and get out of here before the cops come."

"You murdered him!" she moaned. "Oh, you beast! You murdered him!"

The bitter irony of the situation cut Tony to the quick. Reviled by his own sister for having saved her from the rapacity of one of his gunmen! He wanted to take her in his arms, comfort her, explain everything to her, warn her. But he didn't dare. He realized that the knowledge that he was the notorious Tony Camonte would kill his mother. No, his family believed him dead; he must remain dead so far as they knew.

"Shut up!" he commanded with vicious emphasis. "And get out of here!"

Sobbing hysterically, she wriggled into the dress and donned her hat and coat. He took her arm but she flinched away from him and hurried to the doorway. There she paused and swayed unsteadily. Her horrified gaze had seen the bloody heap that was Mike. With a piercing scream she collapsed across the body, frantically kissing the ghastly face.

His own emotions stretched to the breaking point, Tony picked her up roughly and shoved her toward the elevator.

"Get out!" he gritted. "And stay out! And keep your mouth shut!"

She gazed back at him, deathly pale, wide-eyed with terror.

"I hope they hang you!" she cried, and began to run, sobbing in great choking gasps.

She passed the closed elevator door and continued on to the stairway. Tony heard her rapid clicking footsteps and breathless, catching sobs die away. Then he went back and stared down at the body.

"Too bad, Mike," he said in a low tone, as if the inert figure of the dead gangster could hear. "But it had to be done."

He walked into the bedroom and picked up the telephone.

"Mike just died," he said dully, when the clerk answered. "I'll see about arrangements later. Tell all the boys that if some nosy dicks come around, they ain't got the slightest idea what was the name of the dame who came up here tonight with Mike, See? It's curtains for the guy that squeals her name to anybody, hear?" he added viciously. "Tell 'em that, too."

The sharp thud of the telephone as he set it down on the little table penetrated the fog that seemed to have come up around his perceptions since that hoodlum in the lobby had identified Mike's new girl. Well, she was gone now, anyway. If anything happened; she would be clear of it. He realized that the night's events would kill his mother. But she wouldn't know. What a blessing it was that most people actually knew so little.

He walked to the doorway and stared down at Mike's body again. Suddenly his eyes snapped and he hurled the automatic down. It struck the body then bounced away across the hall and lay still, an unerring instrument of death.

The other killings that Tony had perpetrated had given him a thrill, a sharp, exhilarating sense of triumph, of having outwitted and conquered enemies who would willingly have done the same to him. But he felt none of that now. He was dazed, shaky, and very tired. He felt suddenly old. It seemed as if he had lived a century and yet. And yet, it must be less than fifteen minutes.

He turned and went slowly upstairs to his private office. Sinking into the comfortable chair behind his big desk, he rested his elbows on its polished walnut surface and let his head fall forward into his hands.

How long he had been sitting there that way he didn't know. But he realized suddenly that the spacious room was filling with men. He looked up, to find Captain Flanagan, his revolver drawn, staring down at him with a grim little smile lurking around the corners of his hard mouth.

"Well, Tony, I guess we got you this time, with the goods," said Flanagan with relish. "So you killed Mike Rinaldo over a dame."

Tony stiffened and sat up straight, his eyes blazing as he stared at the crowd of officers. Who had squealed?

"Take it easy, Tony," growled Flanagan warningly, sensing the gang leader's sudden arousal. "You're comin' to the D.A.'s office with us. Stick out your mitts!"

There was a metallic rattle as another detective stepped forward with a pair of handcuffs. Tony stared at them. Then an expression of disgust crossed his face and he looked up at Flanagan again with his usual defiant pride flooding back into his face and manner.

"You don't need no bracelets for me!" he snapped. "I'm no cheap second-story man. I'll go with you, anywhere you want to take me,

but I'm goin' to call a mouthpiece to come down and see that I get
my rights."

He reached for the telephone but one of the officers snatched it
away from him. Half a dozen others closed in on him, their attitude
obviously menacing. And Flanagan had lifted the muzzle of his
revolver until it pointed at Tony's chest.

"Oh, you're goin', all right!" said the burly chief of detectives,
seeming oddly elated. "And you're goin' to wear the bracelets. We
ain't takin' no chances. Ain't often we get a chance to pinch a big
shot like you," he added sarcastically, with a nasty grin. "And you
ain't callin' nobody till after you been to the D.A.'s office."

"Listen, Flanagan, I'm due for all the breaks you guys can give
me. The dough I've paid—"

"Don't know a thing about it, Tony," lied the chief of detectives
glibly. "Anyway, I've heard that you haven't been so liberal since
you got to be so strong."

Which was true. Now that he and his gang held undisputed sway
over the booze racket and certain other underworld activities of the
big city, he had trimmed the amounts that he paid out for protection.
No use throwing away any more dough than you had to. If there
were no other gangs that the authorities could throw their allegiance to, they'd ride along for smaller bits.

They handcuffed him none too gently and led him downstairs.
Tony had a glimpse of his gangsters congregating in the lobby staring at the party with amazed hate. And the realization that his men
had seen their master led out by the police, trussed like a common
small-time burglar, galled him much more than the trouble ahead.

He was hurried outside and pushed into one of the three big squad
cars that had brought the party out from the detective bureau and
which were now parked at the curb, guarded by half a dozen other
officers, armed with small machine guns. The whole crowd acted
as if they were executing a coup as daring as kidnapping Napoleon
from the midst of his army.

The three big cars raced downtown, their shrieking sirens clearing
a path and making people turn to stare. Tony's impenetrable silence
masked a seething inward fury. Who had squealed? How had the
dicks known about Mike's death so soon and how had they known
who to pinch for it? It looked as if somebody, seeing a chance to get
him, had taken advantage of the opportunity with all speed. But

who? Well, one thing certain, they'd pay. It would be curtains for the guilty person.

Moran, the first assistant district attorney, was awaiting them in the prosecutor's offices on the second floor of the gloomy Criminal Courts building. And Tony grunted scornfully as he saw him. Moran was a good prosecutor, all right, the best they had; but he was also the collector for his chief. Tony had paid him thousands. He was a tall, lean young man with icy blue eyes behind horn-rimmed glasses, and a nasty, cynical smile that held no mirth in it.

"Well, Camonte, what have you got to say for yourself?" he demanded.

"Nothing—here," snapped Tony. "You must think I'm dumb."

"Yes, I do."

Tony's face flamed and the chain of the handcuffs rattled as his hands clenched and writhed.

"I want to talk to you alone, Moran," he gritted in a low tone.

Moran surveyed him a moment then produced a revolver and laid it on the desk close at hand.

"You fellows can wait in the outer office," he said to the crowd of detectives. "I'll call you when I want you." As they trooped out, he looked up at the gang leader with a deadly glance. "One false move, Camonte," he said coldly, "and I'll shoot you down like a dog."

"Yes, I believe you'd like to get the chance," agreed Tony bitterly.

"It would save the state the expense of trying and hanging you."

Tony laughed harshly. "Don't talk foolish! You couldn't convict me!"

"No? Well, watch us. Or rather, watch me. The Chief says I'm to prosecute."

"Where is he?"

"At home, of course. You're not important enough to get him out of bed in the middle of the night to come down here and question you."

"No? Well, I'm important enough to give him a nice big bit every month. And you, too. If anything happened to me, the gang would go to pieces and you wouldn't get those bits any longer."

"If your gang was broken up, there'd be room for two or three other gangs, and each one of 'em would be glad to kick in with as much as you do. Competition is the life of trade, you know," he added grimly.

"I could increase my bits," suggested Tony shrewdly.

"Yes, but that wouldn't interest us now. Three or four gangs spread around the city are a lot more help to a political machine than just one. And you've never shown any interest in helping us build up the machine, anyway. No, Camonte, this is our chance to knock you off your throne and we're not going to miss it."

Tony's face had frozen and his eyes glittered.

"Listen, Moran," he said, and his voice held a cold, deadly venom that made the assistant district attorney flinch, "if you bring me to trial, you and the D.A. will both be mighty sorry, before it's all over."

"Are you threatening me?" blustered Moran.

"No. Just trying to keep you from making a fool of yourself."

Moran laughed harshly, sarcastically.

"Leave that to us! I'll convict you, all right. The girl's testimony alone will—"

"What girl?" demanded Tony tensely.

"This Rosie Guarino, the one you killed Mike over. She's the one that turned you up for the job and she's volunteered to testify. Women! They're the ruination of all you hoods. I guess you didn't know that this dame and Mike had been secretly married down at Crown Point a week ago."

So that was what they thought, that he had killed Mike because of jealousy. No wonder Flanagan had looked at him with contempt. And she and Mike had been married. Good God! He had had no right to—But how could he know, with Mike's past what it was?

Weary and bewildered, his mind a confused maze, Tony was led away to a cell.

chapter 23

The murder trial of Tony Camonte, the famous gang leader, who had come to be considered beyond the reach of the law, was the sensation of the year. The newspapers found it a godsend during a period when other news happened to be scarce, and devoted their front pages to little else. Public opinion as to Tony's guilt and deserving of punishment was sharply divided.

A certain cross-section of the populace poured down maledictions upon his head and consigned him to the gallows, with sighs of relief. But another group, equally numerous, who through the papers, had followed his daring exploits for years, had come to feel an admiration for this extraordinary man who had risen from vassal to czar. These people openly expressed sympathy for him and the hope that he would be acquitted.

For Tony himself, the period of the trial was a time of soul-wrecking terror. Not because of fear of punishment, for he did not fear it; but because of his overwhelming fear that his real identity would be discovered.

Moran prosecuted, assisted by one of the lesser-assistant D.A.'s, and it was obvious that they were fighting like tigers for a hanging verdict. Tony's defense consisted of two of the most brilliant criminal lawyers in the city, one a former assistant district attorney. And the fee they had already received would enable them to live in comfort for two or three years.

Rosie Guarino was the star witness for the state, of course, but only because Tony chose to allow her to be. His attorneys had relayed to him from his men various proposals for eliminating her from the case, scaring her out of the city, by bombing the Guarino store and home.

They even planned kidnapping. And finally they decided upon a cold-blooded plan for shooting her on the witness stand from the window of an adjoining building.

Tony had angrily vetoed them all, to the bewildered disgust of his lawyers and henchmen. He realized that he could stop her instantly by revealing his identity as her brother, but he was more afraid of that fact coming out than he was of the gallows. He had consented, however, to an offer of fifty thousand dollars being made her to slip out of the city and remain away until he had been acquitted and the case forgotten. This offer she had spurned indignantly and promptly given the facts to the newspapers, thereby furnishing them with another sensational headline. Tony secretly was rather proud of her; she was his own sister, all right.

The whole Guarino family was in court the day Rosie testified. Tony looked at them furtively from his position in the front of the courtroom before the judge. They were all well-dressed and they seemed well and happy. He felt a little thrill of satisfaction. His ill-gotten gains had done them some good anyway; the generous monthly sum that he gave them secretly through an attorney had assured them luxuries and advantages that they never could have enjoyed otherwise.

He saw his mother, dowager-like in a glossy fur coat and a Parisian hat, look at him sharply. For a moment he thought she had recognized him and his heart sank, but he had taken his place so that the throng of spectators could see only the left, the scarred, side of his face. He saw his mother's keen glance turn to contempt and he felt relieved. At that moment he saw himself as others must see him, as a bad boy who hadn't grown up. He was pale and shaken when he turned his attention back to the witness stand.

Rosie gave her testimony with proud defiance and more than one venomous look at him. The prosecution, of course, did not bring out Mike Rinaldo's desperate character, and Tony had forbidden his own attorneys to do so; he refused to stain further the memory of his sister's dead husband. When the state had completed its direct examination of her, one of Tony's attorneys rose for cross-examination.

"Was Mr. Rinaldo completely within your sight from the time he opened the door until you heard the shots and saw him fall?" asked the attorney.

"Yes."

"Didn't you see him suddenly reach for his right hip?"

"Yes."

"Wasn't that before you heard the shots?"

"Yes."

"Then you didn't actually see the defendant shoot Rinaldo?"

"No, but—"

"That's all," said the attorney brusquely.

He turned away then smiled slightly at the sudden stir that appeared at the prosecution's counsel table; the lawyers there were obviously disconcerted by the extreme shortness of his cross-examination of their star witness.

It was plain that Rosie realized she had made admissions damaging to the state's case. She remained in the witness chair, trying to qualify the statements she had made. But a court attendant ushered her out.

There were other spectators in the courtroom that interested Tony. His moll, for instance, Jane Conley, widely known by reputation to police and the underworld as "The Gun Girl," but known by sight to practically none. He was a little puzzled about Jane. She hadn't come near him during his period of incarceration.

As she sat in the courtroom, stylishly dressed and easily the most striking woman in the throng of spectators, she gave him no sign of recognition. He resented her air of detachment.

Yet, wanting to find an excuse for her seeming unfriendliness, he was able to find one. The fact that she was his moll had been kept a close secret and it was better that it remain so. The less that was known about the private affairs of a man in his position, the fewer loopholes his enemies had to try to strike him through.

His brother, Detective Lieutenant Ben Guarino, was a constant and interested spectator at the trial. He was a little surprised at his brother's appearance. Ben had taken on weight and his face looked bloated. He'd been hitting the high spots and it was beginning to tell on him.

The last afternoon of the trial, Tony saw his brother seated beside Jane in the first row of spectators. Occasionally they chatted in whispers and several times he saw them exchange a smile. Jealous rage flowed through the gang leader like molten metal and his eyes blazed. With an effort he turned his attention back to the course of the trial. The climax was approaching rapidly.

In their summation to the jury, Moran and his assistant obviously did their utmost to induce the twelve men to bring in a verdict of murder in the first degree. As they verbally flayed him with all the biting vituperation and sarcastic innuendo of which clever criminal lawyers are capable, Tony found it almost beyond his powers of self-control to remain in his chair. His strong hands gripped the chair arms until his knuckles gleamed white with the effort. His swarthy face flushed to a deep purple and his fingers itched to get at the throats of these hypocrites who characterized him an incorrigible menace to mankind. The automobiles in which they rode, had been paid for with his money.

But he relaxed when his own attorneys had their inning. He even smiled slightly once or twice at some of their cleverly sarcastic quips at the expense of the prosecution. They made the thing out so simply; showed the whole charge to be utterly ridiculous and unproved. They characterized a possible conviction as the most monstrous miscarriage of justice that could ever blot the records of a state. But the jury seemed less interested in the vividly pictured horrors of guilty consciences for convicting an innocent man than they did in the appearance of ten of Tony's best gunmen seated in the first two rows of spectators. They were swarthy, well-dressed young men who surveyed the jurors unsmilingly with cold, hard eyes.

The judge had been paid $10,000 to make his instructions to the jury as favorable as possible to Tony and he went as far as he dared, to earn his fee. The jury required just fourteen minutes to bring in a verdict of "Not guilty." And everybody realized that those ten grimly silent young men had been the deciding factor.

There had been instances where jurors convicting gangsters had been shot, their homes bombed or their children kidnapped. Law and order and duty were all very well, but there was no appeal from a bomb or a bullet. And the law is notoriously lax in protecting its upholders, once their usefulness has ceased.

Tony shook hands with every juror. And some of them were as flustered as though meeting the President. The next day he sent each one a case of uncut whisky.

Tony waited, chatting with his lawyers, until the spectators had dispersed, then he walked out of the courtroom a free man, but a man full of deep grievances that must be avenged.

In the doorway lounged Detective Lieutenant Ben Guarino.

"You'll get yours yet, Big Shot," he rasped.

Tony hurried on without indicating that he had heard. In the hallway, his bodyguard awaited him. Quickly they surrounded him as they had been trained to do and escorted him downstairs and outside to the big sedan with the bullet-proof glass. At a respectful distance watched a crowd that filled the street. The flutter and craning of necks that followed his appearance would have satisfied the greatest celebrity.

Near by a half-dozen newspapermen clamored for an interview and innumerable photographers were frantically trying to snap pictures. Being slightly shorter than the average, Tony purposely had chosen for his bodyguard the tallest men in his mob. Ordinarily they served to protect him from the bullets of ambitious assassins. Now the ring of men served equally well to protect him from the almost as annoying camera lenses. But he spoke to the reporters for a moment.

"I'm through with all the rackets, boys," he announced. "I've got enough money and I'm done. Johnny Lovo had the right idea. I'm going into the real estate business."

He stepped into the sedan and the escort of three cars swept away. Tony Camonte was a czar again.

chapter 24

Tony felt a trifle uncertain as he entered his luxurious Lake Shore Drive apartment half an hour later. And the cool, questioning way in which Jane surveyed him was not reassuring.

"Jeez! I'm tired!" he exclaimed wearily. And he was. The strain of the trial had taken more out of him than he realized.

"Listen, Tony," said Jane, and there was an edge in her voice, "just what is this dame to you?"

"What dame?"

"This Rosie person, the one you killed Mike over."

"She ain't anything to me."

Jane laughed scornfully. "Do you expect me to believe that? Then why'd you bump off Mike for gettin' her?"

"I didn't. It was about somep'm else."

"Don't try to kid me. You and Mike were the best of friends up to the night that happened. The boys say you turned absolutely green when you saw Mike come in with her. Right away you went upstairs and five minutes later Mike was dead."

"You're crazy! I—I never saw her before. If she'd— meant anything to me, do you s'pose she'd have turned me up the way she did?"

"A woman's feelings can change."

"So can a man's." He looked at her narrowly; his tone was significant.

"Yeah? Well, don't worry, Big Shot, there's plenty of men that'd be glad to have me."

"Mebbe. But you'd find it pretty hard to find one that could or would pay the price I do. For the amount I spend on you, I could just about have my pick and don't forget it!"

"Why don't you?" she demanded furiously.

"Been too busy to think about it," he retorted loftily. "But I may not be so busy later on... while we're on the subject, I noticed you were mighty chummy with that dick lieutenant in court?"

"Which one?"

"Were you chummy with more than one? I wouldn't be surprised. But I only noticed one. Ben Guarino, the brother of this dame."

"Oh? So you know all about the whole family, eh?"

"Shut up!" he snarled suddenly, advancing on her menacingly. "I've had all your lip I intend to take."

For a moment they gazed at each other with blazing eyes, their teeth gritted and their fists clenched.

"What's the use of us fightin' this way, baby, as long as we been together?" said Tony finally and his voice was weary. "Honest to God, I never had nothin' to do with that dame. And there's important things to be done now."

"For instance?"

"Gettin' Flanagan and Moran, the damned dirty double-crossers. After all the dough I've paid them! Flanagan could give me a buzz and let me get out of sight that night. But did he do it? No, he comes out himself and nabs me. And even puts the bracelets on me, like I was a common, cheap, petty larceny crook. And Moran, that dirty Irish—"

The oaths crackled off Tony's competent tongue. "Him and that crooked D.A. boss of his. They knew they had a poor case and they knew that Mike's bein' bumped off was a civic improvement. What they shoulda done was forget it. But do they? No, they do their damnedest to gimme the rope because they know they could collect more if there was a lot of big shots in the racket instead of just me controllin' the whole works. Well, I've paid and what did I get? Tramped on, the minute they thought they had a chance to railroad me. Now, they're goin' to pay and pay plenty."

And so they forgot their personal jealousies and differences while Tony outlined his plans for vengeance against those who had betrayed him. But the rift between them had widened. Doubt, once planted, is almost impossible to kill, and upon the slightest provocation can grow with appalling speed into conviction.

Tony went out to his headquarters the next day. And his men greeted his return with the curious silence and the grim, tight-lipped smiles of their kind. But he sensed an uneasiness in their bearing. Something was wrong; he wondered just what it was.

He had not long to wait. Within a few minutes half a dozen of his more prominent henchmen came up to his private office on the top floor of the hotel. One of them, a square-jawed, hard-eyed hoodlum named Finaro, cleared his throat noisily.

"We was wonderin' about that piece in the papers, chief," he began, "about you goin' to quit the racket and go in the real estate business. That was just talk, wasn't it?"

"I haven't decided yet," answered Tony coolly. "I have got enough dough to quit and enjoy life if I want to."

"Yeah. But who helped you make it, chief? We've all had a hand in buildin' up that pile you got. And you owe it to us to keep things movin' and give us a chance to keep gettin' our bit. We've stuck by you through some damn tight times and now when the sailing's easy, you gotta stick by us. If you quit now, the mob'd go to pieces overnight. And then where'd we be? You just can't quit now and leave us in the lurch."

The others nodded in hearty assent as he finished. The man's tone and manner had been respectful enough but his eyes were hard. Tony, his own eyes glowing with inward anger at this first sign of insubordination within the ranks, was about to dismiss them brusquely. But his better judgment told him not to. He sensed an air of menace in the attitude of the group.

He realized suddenly that in organizing and perfecting this powerful gang that ruled the underworld activities of a great city, he had built a Frankenstein, a monster that, acting upon the principles he had instilled into it, would feel justified in destroying him should he attempt to desert now.

In one great vision, he saw that these men felt a loyalty to him only as long as his agile mind planned activities that afforded them a handsome livelihood. The moment his value to them had ceased they would unhesitatingly turn upon him the assassin's bullets that he now could command them to direct at his enemies. He could never quit; they wouldn't let him.

"Forget it, boys," he said, trying to make his tone pleasant. "I was just talking for the benefit of the cops. Carry on everything as usual."

Tony lost no time in carrying out his vengeance upon those who had betrayed him.

For five days he had Captain Flanagan shadowed day and night. Then, with the reports of his spies in hand, he spent two days in working out the actual plan. At last all was ready.

At eleven o'clock one night he had himself driven home to the fancy apartment building where he and Jane lived. He gave the uniformed doorman a cigar and paused a moment to comment on the state of the weather. To the middle-aged, dignified elevator man he gave another cigar and, apparently doubtful of the accuracy of his watch, checked it up with that of the older man. Thus he had impressed his arrival and the time of it upon the two attendants.

His apartment was on the third floor and at the end of the corridor was an iron fire escape that led both upward and downward: Carefully he opened the French doors that gave access to it, stepped out and closed the doors behind him. Then he climbed rapidly but silently down to the ground.

His rubber-soled shoes making no sound, he flitted through the dark alley and stepped into the sedan waiting in the deserted street beyond. The big car sped smoothly away, preceded and followed by another just like it.

At a quiet corner far out on the North Side the three cars paused. Then one proceeded easily through the tree-lined residential street to the next corner. Then another moved slowly forward. In the middle of the block and across the street from a brick two-story house which was still brightly lighted, it stopped against the curb. The four men in it crouched down so that the car appeared empty. Already one of the rear door windows was fully lowered, the cool night air fanning the flushed tense faces of the four men.

Tony waited a moment, then nudged one of his companions. The man lifted a police whistle to his lips and blew three shrill blasts. Almost immediately two shots rang out at the next corner. Abruptly the front door of the house across the street flew open and a burly man emerged, a revolver glinting in his right hand. It was Flanagan!

Another shot rang out at the corner. Flanagan ran down the steps, his revolver ready for action. Slowly Tony lifted the ugly black snout of a sub-machine gun, resting it on the car door, and took careful aim. Then with a grim smile he squeezed the trigger. The death rattle of the weapon deafened him and his companions but Flanagan crumpled to the ground, at least two-score bullets having found their mark in his body. The cars roared away down the street.

Tony went to bed with exultation welling strong within him. He had returned the same way he had departed and, he was positive, without being seen. When the police questioned the attendants of the building as they were sure to do, the two men would earnestly and unknowingly furnish him with a perfect alibi, for there was no other available entrance to the building save the one at which they were on duty.

Flanagan was gone. A score that had been accumulating for years had finally been settled. Now for Moran!

chapter 25

The newspapers the following afternoon gave Tony a shock. The Police Commissioner, in a lengthy statement about Flanagan's daring assassination, said that he felt that younger men were necessary to cope with these modern gangsters, and announced the promotion of Lieutenant Ben Guarino to Captain and Chief of Detectives. The new Chief, in a statement of his own, announced it as his opinion that the affair of the night before was the work of Tony Camonte and his gang, and promised to run Tony out of town or kill him in the attempt.

Tony laughed at that; then he frowned. It wasn't a nice thought to know that your own brother had sworn publicly to hunt you to the death. God! This family mix-up in his affairs was beginning to get on his nerves. Then Tony's jaw set and his eyes flashed. If they ever met in a situation where only one could escape, Ben would be just another dick in his eyes.

Tony went down to dinner in the dining room of his hotel that evening feeling rather well pleased with himself. One of the waitresses came forward to serve him, her crisply-starched white uniform rustling stiffly. He gave his order without looking up. But when she served his soup, her finely manicured hands caught his attention. From the hands, his glance strayed to her figure, the perfection of which drew his gaze upward to the face. Then he almost jumped out of his chair. For the girl was his sister, Rosie.

"You!" he exclaimed.

"Yes," she answered breathlessly in a low tone. "I hoped you wouldn't notice. But I had to do something, now that Mike's dead, and this was all I could find."

She hurried away before he could comment or question her further. Tony dipped his spoon into the soup, then paused. That explanation of her presence here did not ring true. He knew that she did not have to work; the monthly sum he had his attorney send to his family was more than sufficient to take care of them all in luxury.

Then why was she here? Why, indeed, except to attempt vengeance upon him? He gazed at the soup, his black eyes glittering with suspicion. But the clear liquid told him nothing. Surreptitiously he emptied the contents of his water glass upon the floor, and poured some of the soup into the glass. Then he rose and, concealing the glass by his side, walked toward the door that led into the lobby of the small hotel.

"I've been called to the telephone," he explained with a forced smile as he passed her. "Be back in a minute." Out in the lobby, he called one of his henchmen and handed the glass to him.

"Take that over to the drug store across the street right away and have it analyzed," he ordered. "I'll wait here till you get back."

His thoughts in a turmoil, he waited. But he was positive of the verdict even before his henchman returned and breathlessly announced it! The soup contained enough poison to kill a mule, much less a man!

Tony walked back into the dining room with his face an expressionless mask in which only the eyes glittered with life. The nerve of the girl, to get a job in his own hotel so that she could have the opportunity of poisoning him, of exacting the toll for Mike's death that the law had been unable to collect. God! She was his own sister, all right.

He stood beside his table and she came forward, only her flaming cheeks belying her outward coolness.

"You get off at seven, don't you?" he said calmly.

"Yes. Why?"

"I have to go upstairs on business. When you get off, please bring the rest of my dinner up to my private office on the top floor of the hotel. There'll be a big tip in it," he added with an attempt at a smile, "and I want to have a little talk with you anyway."

He went up to his office, wondering if she would come of her own free will or at the behest of the gunmen he had ordered to keep a close watch upon her and bring her up in case she should try to get away without complying with his request. He hoped she would come by herself.

She did, already attired in an attractive street costume, and carrying a large tray with a number of covered dishes. She set the tray down on his desk. He looked up at her grimly.

"Are these things poisoned, too?" he asked.

She jerked so violently that she almost dropped the tray and her eyes widened in terror.

"I don't know what—" she stammered.

"There was enough poison in that soup you served me to kill a dozen men," he continued smoothly. "And they don't usually poison it in the kitchen. So you must have done it."

"Yes, I did," she snapped with sudden defiance. "I loved Mike and you murdered him. You cheated the law but I resolved that you shouldn't cheat me. And I got this job so I could get you. But you've found it out. Now, what are you going to do about it?"

The abrupt directness of her methods, so very like his own, disconcerted him for a moment.

"I haven't decided," he admitted finally. "I ought to have you taken for a ride, but I think you're too brave to be finished up by a stab in the back like that. Do you realize the danger you're in?"

"Yes. I've known all the time what a long chance I was taking. But Mike was dead; what difference did it make?"

"Mike was a hoodlum," snapped Tony harshly. "A gunman and a thug. He'd killed a lot of people and was always ready to kill more whenever I said the word and was ready to pay the price."

"I suppose you think you're better," sneered the girl.

"That's not the question. We're talking about Mike. He wasn't worthy of any girl's love. But I want you to know that I had no idea you two were married. I thought he was just going to take advantage of you, as he had so many other girls. That's why I—I bumped him off."

A tenderness had come into Tony's voice. He caught himself as he saw her staring at him, wide-eyed.

"What's the matter?" he demanded.

"N-N-Nothing. For a minute, you seemed so much like—somebody I—I once knew."

Tony breathed hoarsely for an instant and turned away so that she could see only the scarred side of his face. She had almost recognized him.

"I'm sorry about Mike. But it just had to be," he said doggedly. "And you'll be a lot better off. Some day you'll thank me for what I did. So run along and forget Mike. And from now on, be careful of the guys you pick. You're too nice a girl to be chasing around with gunmen."

"How would you like to mind your own business?" she blazed, her eyes glistening with incipient tears.

"Fine. You might do the same. And don't try to poison any more gang leaders; some of 'em might not like it.... If you need any money—"

"I don't," she snapped proudly. "And I won't. We have plenty."

Tony felt a thrill of satisfaction. They would never know, of course, that their prosperity was due to him. But he was glad that he had been able to make them comfortable.

"All right, then—girlie," he said slowly. "And just remember that you're the only person that ever tried to kill Tony Camonte and lived to tell about it."

Still staring at him curiously, a perplexed frown wrinkling her brows, she finally departed. Tony heaved a long sigh. Well, that was over.

Abruptly he switched his agile, daring mind back to the matter which had become an obsession with him— the wreaking of vengeance upon the officials to whom he had paid so much but who, in time of crisis, had betrayed him. And then he realized that there Was something bigger to all this than venting his personal spite upon these officials who had betrayed not only him but their trust.

For the first time in his hectic life he felt the social impulse which is, at once, the cause and the result of civilization—the realization that the welfare of mankind was more important than his own preservation, the realization that he owed something to the world.

In the grip of new emotions, of strange ideas and convictions hitherto foreign to him, he wrote steadily for two hours. When he had finished he read through the pile of sheets with grim satisfaction, then folded and sealed them, together with a small black leather-covered notebook, in a large envelope, across whose face he wrote: *To be delivered unopened to the* Evening American *the day after my death.* Then he locked it up in his desk.

He realized, of course, the sensation that would follow its ultimate publication but he had no idea that he had just written, with amazing brevity and directness, the most significantly damning indictment of American political machines ever composed. Yet that proved to be the case.

Its publication, unknown to him, was to cause the suicide of half a dozen prominent men, the ruination of innumerable others, a complete reorganization of the government and police administration of not only that city but many others; and, by its revelation to the common voter behind the scenes of activities of so-called public servants, and their close connection with the underworld, was to prove the most powerful weapon of modern times for the restoration of decent, dependable government in the larger cities.

But he would have laughed unbelievingly had anyone told him that now. And he wouldn't have been particularly interested. This social consciousness that had come over him for a time was too new a thing to him to be permanent. Already he was hungry again for action, for personal vengeance against those whom he felt had it coming to them. His cunning mind leaped to the problem which was, momentarily, his main purpose in life—the killing of Moran, that ratty assistant district attorney.

The telephone at his elbow jangled loudly in the complete silence of the room. He lifted the receiver, growled a curt "Hello," and listened to the voice that came rapidly to him with its report. When he hung up, his eyes were sparkling.

Five minutes later, he and four of his most trusted men—that is, best paid—drove away in a high-powered sedan. To the far South Side they drove rapidly, yet at a pace not sufficiently rapid to attract attention. For they were in enemy territory there. If their presence was discovered, a dozen carloads of gangsters, representing the various small and always turbulent South Side mobs—would be gunning for them.

There was danger, too, from detective bureau squad cars. With the contents of his car what it was, Tony realized that it would be impossible for him to give a satisfactory explanation of his presence in enemy territory. And if they should happen to be picked up by a squad that wouldn't listen to reason, they should probably find themselves in a nasty jam.

Across the street from a saloon in a dark neighborhood, they stopped. The engine of their car had been cut off a block away and they had coasted up to their objective, the careful application of their well-greased brakes preventing any sound as they came to a halt. The chauffeur remained under the wheel, ready for the instant getaway that would be imperative, Tony and the other three men slipped on masks that completely concealed their faces. Then, carrying machine guns, they hurried silently across the street.

Noiselessly as ghosts they appeared in the doorway, their weapons poised ready for instant destruction. A score of men were lined up at the bar. And at the end stood Moran, chatting chummily with four men who looked to be very improper companions for an assistant district attorney. In fact, two of them were prominent Irish bootleggers of the far South Side jungles, whom he had prosecuted unsuccessfully for murder not many months before.

The bartender, facing the door, was the first to see the masked intruders as they stood silently side by side with ready weapons. The way he stiffened and stared attracted the notice of the others because they began turning around to see what held his fascinated gaze.

"Hands up, everybody!" barked Tony brusquely.

"My God! It's—" cried Moran, but the rest of the sentence was drowned in the vicious stuttering of Tony's machine gun.

Without so much as a gasp, Moran fell forward, almost cut in two by the hurtling stream of lead. Behind his mask, Tony smiled grimly and swung the spouting black muzzle to include the two Irish bootleggers. Anybody that could stand being chummy with Moran was sure to be a rat and much better out of the way, and these two were notorious bad eggs anyway. As he watched them drop, Tony felt that he had accomplished a civic improvement. And undoubtedly he had saved the state the expense of trying to hang them again at some future time.

Tony loosened the pressure of his forefinger on the machine gun's trigger and the abrupt silence that followed the gun's death rattle was startling.

"Any o' you other guys want a dose of this?" he demanded. The men cowered back against the bar, their lifted hands trembling. "Well, don't come outside for five minutes or you'll get it."

His henchman on the left turned and walked outside, on the lookout for danger from that direction. Tony followed, then the other two men backed out. During the hectic two minutes inside the saloon, the chauffeur had turned the car around and it stood humming angrily at the curb. They all leaped in and it roared away.

Tony was exultant. He had settled all his local scores now, except that with the D.A. himself and the contents of that envelope he had sealed not long before would take care of him—and how! But there was that New York crowd that were trying to invade his domain and who had tried to bump him off just before his trial. Tony frowned and gritted his teeth when he thought of them.

chapter 26

Money will accomplish miracles anywhere, especially in the underworld, and within twenty minutes from the time of Rosie Guarino's departure from Tony's private office, Jane Conley's hired spy had telephoned the information to her. He hadn't been able to give her full details of what had transpired but he could testify that Tony had offered this girl money—which she had refused.

Knowing Tony, Jane felt able to fill in the gaps herself. And it all left her gasping with fury. The fact that she was entirely mistaken in her conclusions made her rage none the less violent. She'd show him that he couldn't two-time her and get away with it.

She was fed up with Tony, anyway. Of late, she had felt an almost irresistible longing for the reckless doings and excitement of her former activities as a gun girl. But Tony wouldn't permit it. As long as she was his moll, she had to stay at home and behave herself. And home life, even in the luxurious abode he provided, had become wearisome.

She had been friendly with only one man. She had always had the retinue of admiring males that surround every beautiful woman, and she missed them now. She felt that she had become entirely submerged to Tony, just another of his many expensive possessions. His supposed philandering was merely the match that set off the powder.

For more than two hours she brooded over it all, then she made up her mind. First she telephoned Captain Ben Guarino, and had a pleasant chat with him. It seemed reasonable to suppose that having the chief of detectives for a boy friend would be a valuable asset to a girl like her. And then she telephoned Tony at his office.

"I've been very busy tonight," he said defensively the moment he heard her voice.

"I'm sure you have," she assented, and he missed the edge in her tone.

"And say, baby, Moran had an accident."

"Really? Were you there?"

"Yeah. Just got back."

"That's splendid. Listen, Tony, I got a real piece of dope for you. That New York outfit has called a big meeting at Jake's Place for midnight tonight. Those big shots from the East are figuring on organizing all the local guys that don't like you—it'll save them the trouble of bringing out a lot of their own muggs from New York."

"Jeez! Baby, where'd you hear that?"

"Never mind! You don't doubt it, do you? Didn't they try to bump you off—

"Yeah, sure," asserted Tony eagerly. "And they're all goin' to be at Jake's Place tonight?"

"Yes. The New York crowd will be in dark blue Cadillacs—three or four carloads of 'em—and they'll prob'ly have the side curtains up. It's only about eleven-thirty now," she continued smoothly. "If you hurry, you might be able to meet 'em on the way out."

"Much obliged, baby. I'll sure do it."

Jane hung up slowly, a grim smile playing about her rather hard lips. If things went right, there'd be a nice story in the morning papers. If it didn't, she'd probably wake up with a lily in her hand. Well, what the hell—a girl only lived once and she might as well get all the kick she could out of life.

Tony's headquarters was humming with activity. Quickly he assembled four carloads of gunmen, gave them strict orders, then climbed in with the group in his personal sedan and the cavalcade raced away.

Jake's Place was a large saloon and gambling establishment catering largely to underworld customers. It was frowsy, sordid and dangerous. Located in a remote, still undeveloped neighborhood almost at the city limits, it was an ideal setting for gangland deviltry. And it had been the scene of plenty.

Tony halted his crew a block away while he took stock of the situation. There were a number of cars parked around the large, frame building but nothing unusual. And he could see no dark blue Cadillacs, either with or without drawn side curtains. Perhaps the boys hadn't arrived yet; midnight was still ten minutes away.

Ah! There they were, a line of cars approaching along the other road that led from the city. In the darkness they looked black but they might be dark blue and they were Cadillacs, all right. There could be no doubt of that. On they came, close together, four of them.

Tony felt his heart leap and his, grasp on the machine gun resting in his lap tightened. This would be the biggest coup of his whole career, proving to the world at large that his domain was his, and his alone, not to be invaded by others, no matter how strong they might be in their own regions.

He snapped out orders in a low, tense tone and sent a man to relay them to the other cars. Four on each side. One each! His plan was simple and direct. His column would move forward, swing into the road beside the other, then rake the enemy with a terrific fire, annihilating them before they could recover from their surprise at the

sudden attack. Each of his cars was to confine its murderous attention to one of the others, the one nearest.

Rapidly his column moved forward and swung into the other road.
Tony lifted his machine gun and squeezed the trigger. The vicious
rat-tat-tat deafened him but he could hear the same stuttering sound
coming from his other cars. Then from the cars of the supposed
enemy, clear and sharp above the firing, came the clang! clang!
clang! of gongs.

"Jeez!" groaned Tony. "It's cops!"

Instead of gangsters, those four cars contained squads of detectives from the bureau. What a horrible mistake! Not that he hated
shooting cops, but because of the consequences that were bound to
fall upon himself and his men. Unless—

Pandemonium reigned. Every one of the eight cars was flaming
with gunfire. The banging roar was terrific. Tony tried to keep his
head in the bedlam. His forces were in a panic; killing officers was
far different than killing enemy gangsters. But there was no back-
ing out now. It was a fight to the death.

His chauffeur, too busy to fight and mindful of his own safety as
well as his employer's, tried to run for it. The big car leaped ahead,
slewed around the first gang car and shot ahead. But one of the
squad cars leaped after, like a spurred horse.

For more than a mile the chase lasted. The cars swayed, swerved,
bounced. Spurts of fire leaped from . gun muzzles in both cars. Two
of Tony's men were unconscious from wounds and another, blood-
covered, was raving incoherently, trying to climb out of the racing
machine. Tony finally lifted a clenched fist and knocked him cold.
He himself miraculously had not been hit. Nor had the chauffeur,
apparently. But that squad car was hanging doggedly to their trail.
Gaining a little, too.

Beside himself with fury, Tony smashed out the back window and
cut loose with his machine gun, the acrid smoke filling his nose and
mouth and making his eyes smart until he could hardly see. The
jolting and high speed made an accurate aim impossible but he
knew that some of his shots landed. And nothing happened. They
must have a bullet-proof windshield. Well, their tires weren't bullet-proof. He depressed the hot, blazing muzzle of the machine gun,
aiming for the tires.

One of them blew out with a bang that sounded above the firing.
The heavy car slewed around and toppled over into the ditch. Tony

gave a hoarse, savage grunt of triumph. But it was short-lived. For at that moment his own car turned over. The chauffeur had mis-judged a turn.

Tony was still conscious when the big car plowed to a stop, rest-ing on its side. But there was no sound from the chauffeur. Tony vindictively hoped the fool was dead.

His head whirling, his breath coming in short, harsh gasps that did not suffice, Tony untangled himself from among the heap of dead and wounded.

Abruptly he stepped back behind the shelter of the car and rested the machine-gun muzzle on a fender. Two men had climbed out of the squad car and were walking cautiously toward him, revolvers glinting in their right hands. His teeth gritted, Tony squeezed the trigger. But nothing happened; it was empty. He drew his automat-ic, for so long his main bodyguard.

Taking careful aim, he fired. One of the men dropped. The other, warned by the shot, threw up his head and lifted his revolver. But Tony only stared, fascinated, while his nervous fingers refused to obey the command that his numbed mind was trying to send. For the man was his brother, Captain Ben Guarino, the new chief of detectives.

Tony saw the revolver flash, then his head snapped back from the impact of the bullet. Anyway, he had always faced it.

Two hours later, Captain Guarino sat in his office at the detective bureau receiving the admiring congratulations of his colleagues and telling them the details of the furious battle which had accom-plished the finish of the notorious Tony Camonte.

"Tony's old moll gimme the tip," he said complacently. "S'pose they'd had a fuss and she wanted to get back at him. She ain't a bad-lookin' dame, either; I met her at Tony's trial. Bet she got a wad of dough and jewelry outa him, too. Anyhow, she gimme a buzz 'bout 'leven-thirty tonight and said Tony and his mob was goin' to pull off a big killin' out at Jake's Place at midnight. And that was my chance to get him with the goods.

"I could see that myself so I got some of the boys and went out. But you know, I can't see what made Tony and his mob start after us the minute they seen us—But God! wasn't it lucky his gun jammed? He was a dead shot, that guy; for a minute I thought sure I was goin' to wake up with a wreath on my chest. But you never can tell about an automatic."

But even an automatic can't jam when the trigger hasn't been pulled.

THE END

LaVergne, TN USA
13 November 2009
164069LV00001B/26/A